I0757353

ORIGIN OF VIOLET

E. N. Chanting

Origin of Violet: A Novella

By E.N. Chanting

©2024

Print ISBN: 979-8-9893509-5-7

E-book ISBN: 979-8-9893509-6-4

TW: Sexual Assault of a minor is discussed (there is no on page assault of a minor), grooming, eating disorder, language, explicit sexual situations, violence, drug use, bloody-murder, death, loss.

Intended for 18+

Thriller, horror, RH romance

Resources: 1-800-THE-LOST

www.missingkids.org

Locks of Love- https://www.locksoflove.org

©2024 E.N. Chanting

Cover Design by Ampersand Book Covers

Edited by J. Tylee Ertel

This is a work of fiction. Unless otherwise indicated, all the names, characters, businesses, places, events, and incidents in this book are either a product of the author's imagination or used in a fictitious manner. Any resemblances to actual persons, living or dead, or actual events is purely coincidental.

ORIGIN OF VIOLET

All rights reserved. Printed in the United States of America. No part of this book may be used or reproduced in any manner whatsoever without written permission except in the case of brief quotations embodied in critical articles or reviews.

AI was not used to create this original work of fiction.

CONTENTS

DEDICATION

To all the lost and broken children who fight back.

CHAPTER ONE

B lood drips from my elbow, making a pattern on the outdated tile floor. The wooden handle of the knife is still gripped tight in my hand. I use the crook of my arm to wipe the splatter of blood from my eyes. My heart sings in my chest. The chaos of my mind settles into a slow rhythm, finally quiet. Peace, I haven't known in a very long time, falls over me and I sigh in relief. Curling up on the floor next to the carcass of the Beast, I drift away, into a dreamless sleep, until my slumber and sense of peace are shattered by a blood curdling scream.

"VIOLET! What have you done!?!"

"What do you mean?" I ask, rubbing the sleep from my eyes.

"What did you do to Jerry? Oh my God! Oh my God! Violet! Oh my God!"

"Stop saying that. I released us from the beast. You should be thanking me, Mother."

She's shaking her head back and forth so fast her skull appears barely attached to her neck. Hmmm, maybe I should help her with that. My lips curl up with glee while picturing the slices I would make into her throat. I don't think this knife would be able to cut through the tendons and bone. I'll have to find something better suited to that kind of carving. Maybe the big, serrated knife she only uses on the turkey at Thanksgiving. I nod to myself, yep, that's probably the way to go.

She dials her cellphone and puts it to her ear. "Y-yes, oh my God, my d-daughter k-killed my husband! He's dead! Please help! I can't. No, I can't. I will. Yes, she's right here. Yes, it's in her hand. Oh my God, there's so much blood. Please hurry, please..."

She bursts into tears and stands there with her phone in her ear. Her eyes are wide, but I don't think she's seeing anything right now. She has a weird, blank look in her glassy eyes. Tears stream down her cheeks and her mouth hangs open, her expression a grimace.

I don't understand why she's so upset. She's free from the Beast too. I would try to explain it to her, but that won't work since she's catatonic. I love that word. I always wanted a cat.

"Mother? Mother?" Yeah, she's no longer on planet earth. That's okay. I'll explain it when she comes back. I smile at her.

My hand is tired of holding the steak knife, so I drop it next to the carcass. I smooth my hair back from my face, smearing the blood on my hand into my blonde locks. I bet it looks pretty in red. I hate having blonde hair. People always say things about my hair. It's long, all the way down my back and it hangs to my ass. I'm not allowed to say ass, but she can't hear me think it. When it's wet, it stretches well past my ass cheeks. It's kind of curly and wavy. More waves at my scalp and then long curls at the bottom. People always say how pretty I am and how beautiful my hair looks. I hate them.

They don't like my eyes though. They say they look 'haunted' or 'disturbed.' One guy told me they're so dark, I look like the devil. Who says those things to a little girl? I actually like my eyes; they match my tainted soul... black as night. I guess I'm not exactly a little girl anymore, I'm twelve. I even got my period last year. That makes me a woman now, right?

I can hear sirens in the distance. I sit on our fancy but faded, cigarette scented sofa to wait. I'm proud of killing the Beast. I have no reason to hide. Looking at Mother, I see she still hasn't moved. Her hand is shaking... the one holding her phone. She's making these weird gasping sounds, sorta like sobbing but quieter. I guess she hasn't realized yet what a great favor I did for her. She will. Then maybe she'll be happy with me.

The blood on my skin is drying. It's pulling my skin as it dries and some of its flaking off. I wonder if you could cook with the flakes. Beast Herbs, it would probably taste like shit. That's another word I'm not allowed to say, ha-ha. *You can't hear me think it, Mother.* My white nightgown is soaked in blood too. It was warm at first, now it feels wet and cold. I never knew blood smelled so much like old pennies. I have a jar of them in my room. They're on top of my dresser next to my Magic-8-Ball.

The sirens stop outside our house. Watching the door while the police bang on it, I see it rattles in its frame. Mother doesn't move or acknowledge the banging.

"It's open!" I holler.

Four men and one woman in uniform come storming inside, guns in their hands. They point them at Mother, and yell at her to put her hands up. She doesn't move. The woman tackles her from behind, then they all rush at her and force her hands behind her back. The woman presses her knee on Mother's back. Mother screams incoherently, she sounds like a wild animal caught in a trap. They check her pockets and bra for weapons, then they take her out of the house. One of the police officers kneels down in front of me.

He looks me over. "Where are you hurt sweetie?"

"I'm not hurt. I killed the Beast. I'm great," I grin at him.

"Okay, just relax, some paramedics are going to come in and check you over. Don't be scared."

"Why would I be scared?" His head tilts as he looks at me, pale brown eyes narrowed.

"Do you want to tell me what happened?"

"Sure," I smile brightly at him. He's nice, I get good vibes from him. He has a wedding ring on his left hand. The top of his head is bald, but he has gray hair around the sides. The best thing are his eyes, they're crinkly and kind. An adult hasn't looked at me with kindness in a long time.

"I got the knife from the kitchen a week ago. I kept it under my pillow. I decided the next time the beast entered my room and came near me, I'd stab him. He came into my room after Mother left this morning. I was asleep so I wasn't ready with the knife in my hand. When I woke up, his hands were on me. I reached under my pillow and grabbed the knife. I told him if he didn't get away from me, I'd stab him. He laughed and didn't let go, so I stabbed him. It went into his shoulder. I ripped it back out and he ran. I caught him in the hallway, and I jumped on his back."

The nice police officer's mouth has fallen open, and his bushy eyebrows are raised, his wide eyes stare at me.

Smiling, I continue, "When I jumped on him, I kept stabbing him. I think I hit one of the big veins in his neck because blood started squirting on the wall. He was trying to knock me off him, but I'm strong and I held on. He fell onto his face. I wanted to make sure he wouldn't live, so I kept stabbing until no more blood squirted out. I was sitting on his back while I stabbed him. The blood splashed me. That's why I have it all over me. Then Mother came back, maybe she forgot something. She screamed at me and called you. That's pretty much everything."

The nice officer looks kind of green and weird. I've never seen a person turn green before, only in cartoons. It's pretty funny looking. He leans back on his heels and closes his mouth.

"Sanders! Get over here!"

A younger guy comes over and looks at me then at the nice police officer. He has red hair. I wish my hair was red, then maybe nobody would say things about my hair.

"What is it, Sir?"

"Please cuff this young lady." He's not looking at me anymore.

He stands up. "Lieutenant?"

"Do as I say, Sanders." The nice bald one turns and walks away. He didn't even say good-bye. That was rude. Maybe he's not nice and was just pretending. I tilt my head and examine the young one, Sanders. He holds his hand palm up and lifts it signaling for me to stand. I hop up and turn around with my hands behind my back. I stand still so he can put handcuffs on me. I don't usually like my hands restrained, but I learned at school, when I used to go, that we can trust the police.

My smile stays bright, I've never been in handcuffs for something I did before. I feel kind of like a badass, I think I should get a tattoo. Maybe one of those tear drops by my eye showing I have one kill. I saw that in a movie once, it was rated R. I wasn't supposed to watch it, but the Beast put it on and didn't let me leave. I'll have to think about it since I like tattoos. Sanders leads me outside to a fire rescue truck. A fireman helps me climb inside the back and has me sit on a stretcher. He has a dog footprint tattoo on his arm. I like it.

"Where're you hurt sweetie?"

"I'm not hurt. The blood is from the Beast."

"What Beast?"

"Jerry, my stepfather. I call him the Beast because he's a monster. Well, he was a monster. Now he's dead." I give him my bright smile. My face is starting to hurt from smiling so much. I don't usually have any reason to smile.

"What's your name sweetie?"

"Violet."

"What's your last name?"

"Paredes."

"How old are you?" he asks.

"Twelve."

"This might hurt a little. It's going to squeeze your arm so I can take your blood pressure, okay?"

"Sure." He wraps a black band around my upper arm and closes it with Velcro. He pumps it up until it squeezes my arm hard. Then he listens to my arm with a stethoscope. He writes down everything I tell him and my blood pressure. He puts a thermometer in my mouth and takes it out when it beeps. He writes that down too.

"Do you know how much you weigh?"

"Nope."

"How tall you are?"

"Nope."

"Officer? Hey, can you please uncuff her?" The woman officer climbs into the truck and uses a key to unlock one cuff. She hooks it onto the stretcher. My left wrist is now cuffed to the makeshift bed. She sits down and stares at me.

"Violet, do you know if you have any allergies or any medical conditions?"

"No."

"Do you take any medication on a daily basis?"

"No." I don't know if they like my answers, but I love the attention.

"Okay, I'm going to step outside for a minute. Officer Harrison, is going to stay with you."

"Sure." I keep smiling at both of them.

Officer Harrison looks at me with her head tilted down and her eyes narrowed. Her nose is scrunched like she smells something bad. Maybe I stink, or maybe she's just repulsed by me. I don't care, my smile never falters. Maybe she's just having a bad day. I imagine she might have stubbed her toe after climbing out bed, then she burned her tongue on her coffee. Now she's hungry for lunch, but she can't eat because she has to be here with me. I imagine her smiling at me, much better.

The fireman returns and Officer Harrison leaves. He does some paperwork, then he looks at me again.

"Do you want to harm yourself?" he asks.

"Of course not. That would be dumb."

He smiles, "I have to ask. Do you feel safe at home?"

I laugh, "I do now."

"Okay, I guess that's it. We're going to transport you to Mystic Cross Medical Center to have you evaluated. It's a short drive. I just have to fasten your seatbelt."

"Yeah, okay." He fastens a thick belt across my waist. He tightens it so I can't move at all. I lean back against the raised head of the stretcher. He taps on the wall to the cab of the truck.

The truck starts moving and I quietly sing a song to pass the time, it's my favorite song, *'Sweet, but a psycho...'*

CHAPTER TWO

I stretch out on my clean white bed and in my soft new hospital gown. The nurse even gave me a scrunchie for my hair. I feel relaxed and comfortable. The doctor is supposed to come see me soon. They already had me pee in a cup, poked me for blood, and looked at my whole body. The nurse was nice and told me each thing she was going to do, but it was uncomfortable when she stuck a metal thing inside me. She took pictures of my privates too, that was embarrassing. She also took pictures of me from the front and back, naked.

I've had naked pictures taken before, but it was the Beast or his friends that did it and they weren't nice... they hurt me. I'm not sure what to think about the nurse. She promised the pictures would be private and only the doctors would see them. I closed my eyes, so I didn't have to watch. I pretended I was a model at a photo shoot for a magazine. It was very quick. Jerry and his friends would make me pose for hours. They didn't care if I got tired. They would hit me or pinch me if I didn't do what they told me. The nurse didn't hurt me at all, except with that metal thing. The nurse gave me a stuffed teddy bear to hold while she did the metal thingy. It helped a little.

The door swings open with a knock. "Hi Violet, I'm Dr. Nercy. How're you feeling?"

"I'm okay. I like the hospital nightgown."

"Are you hungry?" he asks.

"Yes! I haven't eaten anything since lunch yesterday." He writes something on his notepad. He's tall, with dark hair. His eyes are pale blue, and they seem emotionless. Not kind, not cold, just blah. I hope he'll be nice to me like the nurse.

"I want to talk with you about what happened this morning, okay?"

"Yeah." I don't mind telling them over and over about destroying the Beast. I'm proud of myself for doing it without anyone's help.

"I would like for you to tell me what happened from the time you woke up."

"I already told the police officer. Didn't he tell you?"

"He did. But I'd like to hear it directly from you, all right?"

"Oh, okay." I tell him everything I told the green officer. He doesn't turn green. In fact, the expression on his face doesn't change at all. I can't tell whether I should like him and trust him or not.

"You said the Beast had his hands on you. You mean Jerry Raider, your stepfather?"

"Yes."

"Is that the first time he ever put his hands on you?"

"No, like I said, I got the knife from the kitchen a week ago because I was going to make him stop. I thought you had to be smart to be doctor." I rolled my eyes at him. They must let everyone do what they want now.

"Yes, well, ahem. Does your mother know what your stepfather did to you?"

"I told her, but she doesn't believe me. She says that the Beast is the best thing to happen to us, and I need to respect him and follow his rules. We used to live in a really small trailer house. Mother always had a bunch of men over, but once the Beast started coming over the others stopped. I liked that because some of those strangers looked at me weird or tried to touch me. Mother wouldn't let them if she was awake. Then she married him, the Beast I mean, and we moved into his house. She thinks it's great, but she's not home much. I'm the one who has to be there with him and his friends. It's not great, not even close."

"How old were you when your mother married Mr. Raider?"

"Six," I replied.

"What about your father? Where is he?"

"Mother says I don't have one. Obviously, I have a sperm donor, but I don't think she even knows who he was," I shrug.

"Do you ever hear voices? In your head or out loud?" he asks.

"I hear my own voice in my head. Is that what you mean?"

"That's fine. What about hallucinations? Do you ever see things that aren't really there?"

"How would I know that? If I see them, then to me they're there, right?" I shake my head. Is he serious right now?

"Have you ever seen something that other people around you can't, see?"

"I don't know. I've never seen something that later I found out wasn't there. Does that help?"

"Yes, that's fine. Do you ever cut yourself?" he asked.

"On purpose? No. On accident, yeah, sometimes."

"Do you ever want to hurt yourself? Do you think about dying?"

"I think about living, despite the people hurting me," I raise my chin.

"What grade are you in at school?"

"I don't know. I don't go to school anymore," I slump.

"Why not?" he was getting on my nerves with these questions.

"The Beast decided I should be home schooled, but neither he nor Mother teach me anything from school. He was training me, he said, but he never taught me any math or science or anything.

But I teach myself. I'm allowed to go to the library once a week because I can walk there. I'm allowed to go for one hour. They let me check out 30 books at a time. So, I read and teach myself. I love the library!"

I smile thinking about the library, it's my favorite place. Little Women is my favorite book, so far. I want to read them all, but I don't think that's possible.

"I'm going to give you some tests tomorrow. We'll evaluate your grade level and your intelligence. The tests will be on a computer. How does that sound?"

"Great, I love tests. I haven't had any for a long time. Thank you."

He scribbles on his pad. He looks at me for a minute, examining me, I guess. His mask never changes.

"Okay Violet, I'll have them bring you a tray of food. Relax. Watch some television. I'll see you again tomorrow, okay?"

"Okay, goodbye Dr. Nercy."

"Goodbye, Violet." The doctor leaves the room, leaving me alone with the T.V. all to myself.

CHAPTER THREE

What they gave me yesterday wasn't very good, but this breakfast is delicious. I've never had French toast before. It's so good, with butter and syrup...mmm. The Beast never let me eat sweets. He told Mother I wasn't allowed any sugar because it would make me fat. I think I'm pretty skinny. I looked at my chart when the nurse was busy, and it says I'm five feet five inches tall and I weigh one-hundred-eight pounds. I'm not sure if that's skinny or not, but I can see my hip bones and my ribs stick out.

My chest is kind of big, and my ass is big, I think. It's hard for me to tell. But my clothes are always kind of tight around my hips and chest but loose around my waist. Lucky me, I don't have to worry about it anymore. The Beast is dead! I can have sugar, I'm so happy!

As I shovel the last bite into my mouth there's a knock on the door and Dr. Nercy comes back again. He looks exactly the same as yesterday in his white coat, but he has on a pink shirt today. He looks at what I'm eating and writes a quick something in his notebook.

"Good morning, Violet, how are you feeling today?"

"Mmmm, so good. This French toast is amazing."

"I see you've cleaned your plate. The nurse told me you ate about half of your lunch yesterday, and most of your dinner. It's good that you have an appetite."

"Okay..." I push the empty tray away from my stomach and keep the chocolate milk.

"We're going to do the test that I talked about yesterday. Are you ready to take it?"

"I have to pee. Is that okay?"

"Of course, go ahead and I'll be outside your door at the nurse's station. Just come out when you're ready."

"Sure, Dr. Nercy. I'll be out in a minute." When I step out, Dr. Nercy lifts his head and watches me. Then he stands and signals me to follow him.

The hallway smells like cleaning chemicals, and I wrinkle my nose at it. The floor is shiny, but ugly, and it's an ugly pale green. There are machines up and down the hall and a few patients walking, holding onto poles with a bag of liquid hanging at the top. A few are in wheelchairs. Some nurses and doctors rush by while others slowly assist patients.

"Come this way, Violet. I have your test ready in the office. Like I explained yesterday it will be on a computer. Have you used a computer before?"

"All the time. I'm allowed to use the one in the office at home if the Beast isn't using it. It's another way I teach myself. I read and watch videos. I also taught myself how to do some coding and play video games. The Beast doesn't like me playing video games because I can talk to other people, but if I keep it muted, I'm allowed to play. I love Minecraft."

"This should be pretty familiar to you, then. It will ask a group of questions and when you're finished it will switch to another group of questions. I'm going to stay in the room so if you have any issues or need to use the restroom, you can just let me know."

"Okay." I wonder if he'd let me game after this. Probably not.

We enter a small room with a computer desk against the wall. There's a table in the middle of the room with four chairs. The doctor has me sit at the desk. The screen is on and says, *Start*, in the middle. The metal of the chair is cold on my legs.

"You can click on start when you're ready. I'll be right over here at the table. Let me know if you need anything and when you're finished. Just give the best answer you can for each of the questions."

"Yeah, okay."

I click on it and the test opens, showing one question per screen. Some of the questions are really dumb. I have to answer math questions and choose the correctly spelled word out of four options. Then I have to choose the sentence that is grammatically accurate. As I click each answer the test gets harder. The longer I go on, the more I like it. I hate stupid questions.

After a while, it starts asking how I feel about certain things and there are multiple choice answers about how I would react in various situations mixed in.

"Violet?"

I turn and look at him, "Yes?"

"I'm going to step out for a moment, will you be alright on your own? Do you need anything?"

"I'll be fine, but I'd really like a glass of water, please."

"Sure, I'll get one while I'm out. Don't leave this room. I'll be back in just a few minutes." He leaves and the room, closing the door quietly behind him.

I turn back to the test and continue answering the endless questions. When I finish a calculus equation, the test ends. Finally! That wasn't as fun as I hoped. I fiddle with the computer and find it's connected to the internet. I sign into my personal account and open Minecraft. While I play, I find some settings and reconfigure the computer, so it has pretty pictures and music playing in the background, then I quickly hack into my medical record. This hospital needs better cyber security, it was way too easy. I thought my records would be better protected. When the photos of my body pop on the screen I quickly click them away. I read what Dr. Nercy's said about me:

"Summary of findings- The patient is underweight. The patient is calm and in good spirits. The physical examination showed evidence of long-term sexual and physical abuse. There are varying stages of healing bruises on breasts, quadriceps femoris, pharynx/cervical spine, and dorsal posterior. The internal exam showed additional bruising to vaginal walls and cervix, hymen is not intact, and there is minor tearing to vagina and more extensive tearing of anus and rectum." He adds all this to his notes from the other day.

"Patient denies visual or auditory hallucinations. Patient denies self-harm or suicidal ideology. Patient reports she has not attended formal school 'in years'. Patient reports she has been 'teaching herself'. Patient appears unaffected by the loss of stepfather, and reports feeling 'happy that she stabbed him.' Patient appears indifferent to the horror of the scene. The patient was covered in victims' blood upon arrival and voiced no concerns regarding her state. Patient indicates stepfather is responsible for her injuries and she has been abused by stepfather since age six. Evaluation of intelligence and grade level will be completed by use of the Manchester Standard Psychometric and Rengrave Emotional Quotient tests respectively. A psychosocial evaluation will follow.

No therapeutic or pharmaceutical intervention indicated at this time."

Hmm, I'm not sure what all of it means, but I get the general idea. Seems the tests will decide what they do with me and if I need medication or therapy.

The doctor returns with a bottle of water in his hand, and I exit back to Minecraft. He looks over my shoulder at the screen. "What are you doing? How did you get to that screen?"

"I finished the test, so I decided to play Minecraft. I just clicked on the internet and signed into my account."

"I was told there was no internet access on this terminal."

He scratches his head and looks at me with his eyes wide and his lips puckered to the side. I smile.

"I'm all done. Is it lunch time yet?"

He shakes his head a bit and inhales deeply.

"Yeah, sure. I'll take you back to your room. You can have lunch and then I have another test where I'll ask you questions. We can do that this afternoon. Here's your water, come on," he says handing me a bottle.

I completely sign out and return the computer to my finished test. I don't know how I know all the things I can do on a computer. I get a feeling, or an idea, and I try it. Most of the time it works the way I want. I read a few coding books and that got me started. Once I understood the logic of the codes, I was able to write my own. It all comes pretty easy to me. Now I can do just about anything I want on a computer with internet access. If it doesn't have access, I can usually connect anyway if it's available. I open the water and take a few gulps, then I follow the doctor.

When we pass the nurse's station by my room he leans over the desk and very softly says to the nurse there, "Megan, I need you to get a hold of Amar, please. I need to speak with him about the testing terminal right away. Thanks." He looks back at me and I'm pretending to be interested in a poster that identifies the symptoms of a heart attack and the steps to help someone who's having one.

"Come along, Violet. This is your room."

He points to a door a few more steps away from the nurse's station. I enter and my bed's been made. There's a pitcher of ice water on the table, and a man sitting in the chair. He has gray-streaked brown hair and is wearing a long sleeve button down shirt and tie. There's a badge at his waist and he's wearing a holster, but it's empty.

"I'm Dr. Nercy, and you are?" the doctor says, holding his hand out towards the man. The man stands shifting some folders and a notebook. He reaches out his right hand, shaking the doctor's.

"Detective Martinelli, I'm here to interview Miss Paredes."

"Doesn't her guardian have to be present?" The Detective pulls a paper from the top folder. He hands it to Dr. Nercy, who looks it over.

"That is a signed parental release allowing me to speak with her without a guardian present."

I speak up, "I want a lawyer." I've read enough to know my rights.

"I'm sorry Detective Martinelli, regardless of her mother giving you permission, I believe Miss Paredes is entitled to have legal counsel present during any questioning once she's requested a lawyer. Miss Paredes is only twelve, and she's been a victim of long-term abuse. I can't allow you to speak with her without her interests being secured."

The Detective frowns and his eyebrows scrunch together. He looks the doctor over. To me he appears to be looking for a weakness. Dr. Nercy stands his ground, his face is stern, his shoulders move back; he doesn't budge.

"Ahem, Dr. Nercy, this is highly unusual. I have a legally executed document allowing me access to Miss Paredes. I'm going to have to speak with the Hospital Director."

"Do whatever you feel you must, Detective. I'm responsible for my patient's well-being which includes her safety, even preventing her rights from being violated, and I feel that I'm doing my job." They stare at one another for a moment. The doctor places his hand on my chair and steps between me and the Detective.

"Very well, Dr. Nercy, you give me no choice. I'll be in touch. Good day, Miss Paredes."

The Detective steps around Dr. Nercy and exits the room. When he's gone Dr. Nercy looks at me. I release my breath.

"Wow, that guy's an asshole. Thanks Dr. Nercy. Do I actually have a lawyer?"

"You're welcome, Violet. And I don't know. I'm going to have to make a few calls. I'll get someone to bring in your lunch. Don't worry about this. If I have to, I'll stay with you while he talks to you. Go ahead and relax, watch some T.V. and enjoy your lunch."

"Okay." I smile at him. I think I like him. That was very cool. He didn't have to stand up for me or make calls on my behalf, and now, he just earned my trust. I climb onto my bed and wait for my food.

CHAPTER FOUR

Nurse Lindsey brings in a young guy with dark hair and dark eyes carrying a laptop. She introduces him.

"This is Amar, he works in our IT department. Dr. Nercy said he could speak with you." He smiles at me with bright white teeth. He appears harmless, but I'm not a fan of strange men, especially in what is basically my bedroom. She sees my hesitation and she gives me a reassuring smile.

"I'll leave the door open, and I'll be right outside, if you need me."

"Yeah, okay, I guess."

"Hi Violet, may I call you Violet?" He has a nice accent; it makes his voice sound musical. I want hear him talk some more.

"It's my name."

He chuckles, "Right. I wanted to talk to you about your computer test earlier."

I nod. "Okay."

"Dr. Nercy said you were playing Minecraft on the terminal when you finished your test. How did you get the internet to work on that computer?"

"I just typed into the terminal and connected to the internet and went to my account on Minecraft and signed in to play."

"How did you, or rather, what did you type to connect to the internet?"

"I just clicked on the settings and connected to the Wi-Fi, then went online and signed into Minecraft, like I said."

"Let me try it another way. How did you know to do that?" he asks.

"I didn't. I just tried it and it worked."

"I don't think I'm asking this right. If I gave you this laptop, could you show me what you did?"

"No. My lunch is here." I look behind him at the cafeteria guy in a hair net who has my food on a tray. He pushes the table with wheels over to me and places my tray on it. It's a sandwich and potato chips, what looks like potato salad, and root beer. Maybe it's a brownie I see in a bowl wrapped with plastic. This doesn't look too bad.

"Oh, um, yeah, okay. Maybe I can come back later, and we can talk some more?"

"I guess," I told him. I hope he doesn't come back. He asks too many stupid questions.

I bit into my sandwich and ignore him. He seems nice enough, but I've read that you should never admit to hacking, and never ever show anyone how you do it. I won't be answering his questions, at least not in any way that might be helpful. But I might talk to him enough to enjoy his voice. I also don't see Dr. Nercy the rest of the day. The nurse, Michelle, tells me he left word he'll see me in the morning. It's fine. I'm tired from all the questions anyway. I'm bored, and I want to get out of here. But I have to wait for them to finish all of their tests.

I flip channels on the TV until I find Street Racing with Wizard. It's my favorite show. I love all the fast cars; they're so cool. I want a Mustang when I'm old enough to drive. I want an old one, like from the 1990's. I want to fix it up, so it goes fast, and I want to make it really pretty. I want a custom paint job. Purple is my favorite color, so I want sparkly purple paint with a mural on the hood. I want Pegasus flying in a dark night sky with the moon and stars.

I fall asleep and dream of riding a flying horse. I'm so disappointed when Nurse Marilyn wakes me to take my blood pressure and temperature. There's no flying steed tied to the foot of my bed. When she's finished, I try to continue my dream. Unfortunately, I dream about beasts and monsters chasing me. They restrain me and hurt me, and I wake up with a scream. It takes me a moment to remember where I am and why. Oh yeah, the Beast is dead. Nurse Marilyn throws my door open and turns on the light, blinding me.

"What happened? Are you all, right?"

My arm quickly covers my eyes. "I'm fine, just a nightmare. Any chance you could turn out the light?"

She flips it off. "Sorry dear, you scared me. If you're okay, I'll leave you be."

"What time is it?"

"It's 5 a.m. Do you need something?"

"No, thanks, I'm just going to go back to sleep."

"All right, sweet dreams." She closes my door gently, and it bothers me. I feel restless, like I want to cut someone. It felt really good ending the Beast. There're lots more monsters like him who need to be dispatched. I wonder how I would find them. I want to find the Beasts friends who've hurt me and stab them too. But then I want to find more monsters and stab them all. I'm going to have to think on this for a while. I guess I fell back asleep because I jolt awake when there's a knock on my door, as it opens, Dr. Nercy enters.

"Good morning, Violet. How are you feeling?"

"Like I need the restroom."

"I have someone here to meet you. Go ahead and do what you need to do. I'll be right back." He walks out, and I get up to take care of business.

When the door opens again, Dr. Nercy enters followed by a younger man. He's tall with auburn hair, amber eyes that are an interesting gold color, and his face brightens with a smile.

"Violet, this is Krewe Krowley. He's an attorney, and he's agreed to help you."

"Hi." I lift my hand in a lame wave. I don't know what to say.

"It's nice to meet you, Violet. Dr. Nercy has told me about your situation, and I want to help."

"Help with what exactly?"

"The State Attorney's office has filed first degree murder charges against you. I'm going to represent you, and hopefully help you avoid going to jail." I think about this. I understand what first degree murder is, and I know the penalty is life in prison or death by electric chair. I'm not sure how a victim of horrific abuse can be charged with first degree murder, but I'll let Krewe explain it to me.

"How are you going to do that?"

"For one thing you're a minor, so that'll help mitigate the way they can prosecute you. We can also prove the abuse you endured. Lastly, due to the abuse, I believe we can claim temporary insanity." I nod, as his arguments make sense to me.

"I'm your attorney as soon as you hire me," he chimes. As if I could afford it.

"I don't have any money."

"Oh, Violet, I found this five-dollar bill, that you dropped. Krewe has agreed to accept it as his retainer. Here you go, just give it to him and tell him you're hiring him," doctor Nercy places a five-dollar bill in my hand, and he winks at me. Ah, I understand. I read a book once where a kid hired an attorney for a dollar. I take the bill and hold it out towards Krewe.

"Mr. Krowley, I'd like to hire you as my attorney. Will you please accept this five dollars as a retainer?"

"Yes, Miss Paredes, I accept. I'm your attorney now. Good job. Please call me Krewe." He brings out my brightest smile. I like him, and I trust Dr. Nercy. If he trusts Krewe, I'm going to trust him until he gives me a reason not to.

"Please, call me Violet. What happens now?"

"I have a lot of work to do Violet. You're going to do what Dr. Nercy recommends. You're not going to talk to anyone about what happened unless I'm present. Especially, don't say anything to the police. The police are *not* your friends. They're allowed to lie and trick you, so don't ever trust them. They use tactics that are reprehensible to manipulate people into confessing."

"I already told the green cop what happened." Though now I'm realizing that was a bad move.

"Green cop?" his head tilts in confusion.

"He didn't tell me his name. Then he turned green when I told him what I did. So that's what I call him."

"Did he read you your rights?"

"That Miranda warning, right?"

"Yes."

"No, no one has said those words to me."

"Then we can get anything you've said up to now, thrown out." He smiled at me, looking relieved.

"Great. You and Dr. Nercy have to keep my secrets, right? Because of confidentiality." I ask.

"Not Exactly," Krewe shuffles his feet, "It's complicated. It's best if you don't discuss the details of what happened with anyone. I can defend you without knowing and Dr. Nercy doesn't need to know what happened that day to treat you, for now."

"Okay. I won't talk about what happened to the Beast with anyone."

"Great. You can talk about everything that happened before that with Dr. Nercy, so he can treat you. You can tell me about it if you want to as well, but it's not necessary right now." Krewe clears his throat and he and Dr. Nercy exchange a look I don't understand. But I like him, he's nice.

"Dr. Nercy has given me the results of your tests so far. You're an extremely intelligent young lady. Your tests indicate you're at a college level, academically of course. You also show significant impacts from the trauma of the abuse you've been through. I know that's not a good thing, but it's good for your case." Krewe continued.

"Why's that?" How can anything left by the Beast and his friends be a good thing?

"If they continue to pursue first degree murder charges, the death penalty or life in prison could be the sentence. If you're found to have been temporarily insane, they can't sentence you with either of those. I'm going to argue your age, the abuse you've suffered, and as a last resort, temporary insanity. I think we have a good chance to prevent you going to jail at all. Do you understand?"

"Yeah. What about my mother? She hasn't spoken to me at all. I told her several times what the Beast was doing to me, and she wouldn't believe me. She said if any man touched me, it was my own fault. That *I* caused it by being a little slut. I don't want to speak to her, but I thought she would come here and yell at me at the very least."

"Unfortunately, she's acting as a witness for the state, against you. She's filed paperwork to relieve her of parental responsibility for you," Dr. Nercy explains.

"I'm filing paperwork to have you emancipated. That means you won't need parental permission for anything, and you'll be responsible for yourself. I'm not sure if that will go through because of your age. Most emancipation cases involve older teens, usually at least 16 years old. But with your intellect, we may be able to get it approved." Krewe adds.

"Wow, it sounds like you've already done a lot of work. Thank you, Krewe."

"I'm happy to do it. I think your imminent arrest is a travesty. I have an interest in helping victims of crimes, wrongful accusations, and prosecution."

"When will I be arrested? What'll happen then?"

"I'm going to be here, but Dr. Nercy won't release you. They'll photograph you and fingerprint you. They'll probably want to handcuff you, but you'll stay in the hospital. We may have you moved to Mystic Cross Gardens, the psychiatric center; it'll bolster our case. We're going to do our best to prevent you going to jail. If you have to go, it'll be to the juvenile facility."

Dr. Nercy speaks up, "The detective has called already this morning to schedule a visit to interview you. I'll let you know what time we agree upon. He'll likely bring the warrant for your arrest and formally arrest you when he gets here."

"Okay, thanks." I smile at them, not sure what else to do.

"Okay! We're going to get busy. Dr. Nercy will let you know what's happening and when. Here's my card. You can call me any time, day or night, if you need anything. They have to allow you to call me. Remember not to say anything to anyone about what happened. No matter what, *don't* say a word to the police. Got all that?" I nod. "Any questions?"

"Nope, I'm good. Thank you." I look down at his card, trying to memorize the number.

They say goodbye and leave my room, presumably to work on the things we talked about. It's weird but I'm not worried. I trust them and I don't believe I'll get the death sentence or any sentence really. I think about Mother. I'm not surprised she would try to ditch me. She probably would've done it a long time ago if it weren't for the Beast wanting to keep me. Good riddance! I'd still like to help her with her wobbly neck. A sinister grin corrupts my face, and it feels *good.*

I wander to the small library at the end of the hall. There's not much selection but I find a book that looks interesting. I take it back to my room and pass the time reading. It's a strange story about vampires who play baseball and go to high school. But it's entertaining, that's all I need.

Sometime after lunch, nurse Lindsey comes into my room. She checks my vitals and tells me Dr. Nercy is coming in about half an hour to finish my tests. I find myself anticipating his arrival probably more than I should. It's boring here, so even being asked a bunch of lame questions sounds like fun.

Dr. Nercy arrives with a knock on my door, and he opens it like usual. He gets right to business asking his questions. When he's finished, he explains that Detective Martinelli will be here at 6 p.m. to interview me. Krewe will also be here. He wants me to eat before they arrive, so he calls for my dinner to be delivered by 5 p.m.

At 5:15, my dinner is delivered by the same cafeteria guy. I know he works in the kitchen because he wears a hairnet. It isn't becoming, and he's a very large man, so a hairnet looks kind of ridiculous on him. He's always nice to me, bringing me chocolate milk with every meal, and I love it. He winks at me when he puts my food tray on the wheeled table that stretches over me and the bed. I grin in return.

I eat quickly. It's some type of chicken that's breaded. There are cheesy potatoes that taste good, some salad, and corn round out the meal. There's a package of three cookies for dessert. When I finish, the nurse takes my tray and tells me Dr. Nercy is outside doing paperwork and will be in shortly.

He enters with his usual knock and Krewe follows behind him. They greet me and sit in extra chairs that have been brought in. Not long after, Detective Martinelli arrives and before he sits, he gives my attorney the warrant for my arrest. Then he tells me I'm under arrest and he reads my Miranda Rights from a small card, though he doesn't look at the card. A female uniformed officer comes in and takes my photo and fingerprints; it's all very quick.

Then the detective starts asking questions. I answer some and ignore others. I follow Krewe's advice which he gives me by nodding or he challenges Detective Martinelli and tells him no. It's pretty entertaining. When he's finished, the Detective argues with Dr. Nercy about leaving me cuffed to my bed. Dr. Nercy won't allow it because of my traumatic past. He says they can't restrain me because I've been abused with restraints. Detective Martinelli decides to place an officer at my door to guard against my escape, and I roll my eyes at him. Where would I go and in a hospital gown no less? Whatever.

When he leaves, Dr. Nercy and Krewe discuss what's next. They plan to place me in Mystic Cross Gardens in a few days. They have some arguments to file with the court first. Especially the emancipation papers. I'll need to find some patience. Once they leave, Nurse Michelle comes in and lets me shower while she changes my sheets. She sneaks me some ice cream and admonishes the officer outside my door for leaving it open. Once she's gone, he comes into my room.

"Hi, Miss Paredes, I'm Officer Blake. I'll be out here if you need anything. I wanted to introduce myself, so you won't be scared of me."

"Why would I be scared of you? Are you a bad guy?" His eyebrows pop up and his eyes go wide. I guess I surprised him.

"No, I just didn't want to be a total stranger. Okay... Uh, I'll be here. Just call out or come get me if you need anything."

"Sure." His cheeks get pink, and he looks down. I think I embarrassed him, interesting. He's an adult, I'm twelve... really dude? I shake my head and get back to watching a true crime show. I think about moving to the psych ward. I wonder what that'll be like. Krewe said it'll be a few days until he has answers from the judge. Come on patience, come find me.

CHAPTER FIVE

I'm moving to the psycho hospital today. The judge didn't accept the motion to drop the charges. He did accept the emancipation filing, I'm my own person at age twelve, I can speak for myself without a guardian. That's pretty incredible, but who's going to listen to me? I can enter foster care if I'm not in jail. They probably shouldn't trust me to be any place without a lock on the door. I have plans for those who've harmed me, including Mother.

Nurse Lindsey puts me in a wheelchair. I argue, but she explains we have to go clear across the campus to enter a different building for the center, so she's required to transport me in a chair. Some rules are really stupid. My overly friendly guard walks with us. I've learned his name is Christian Blake, he's twenty-two, and he has his own apartment. He has a younger brother who's fifteen and looks nothing like him. He showed me a picture of the blonde haired, light eyed, gangly man-boy. His father is dead, and his mother is mad at him for joining the police force. He gets bored sitting in the hall, so he opens the door and talks to me. The nurses won't give him the time of day, but I'm a captive audience.

We're required to be escorted through two security doors to enter the psycho ward. A woman dressed in blue scrubs greets us and checks my paperwork.

Then she asks, "Do you have anything with you? Personal items? Eyeglasses? Shoes?"

Nurse Lindsey answers for me, "All of her clothing including her shoes was confiscated by the police."

"Okay we'll stop at the closet. I've got it from here." Nurse Lindsey wishes me luck and leaves with the wheelchair. I follow the unnamed woman into my new home.

I'm going to stay in the children's unit. I have a roommate. She's in our room when I arrive, and stares at me and Officer Blake who continues to follow me. He sets up outside my door, which I don't understand. I'm under lock and key here, why is he needed?

My roommate is incredibly thin and tiny, with short dark hair and pretty brown eyes. Her eyes are a bit large for her face, but she's very pretty. They don't look *that* weird. She watches as I put away my new wardrobe of five sweatpants, two pairs of shorts, seven bras, seven panties, seven pairs of socks, seven t-shirts, and one hoodie.

"Hi, I'm Violet. What's your name?" She looks me over and I can almost hear the gears churning inside her head. I'm being evaluated and judged. While she decides if she's going to answer, I look over my bed and the general décor. It's nice. It fits with the *hip teen* vibe they're trying for in the hallway. Dr. Nercy told me this place is for very rich kids with very big problems. Lucky me, it's the only facility within a hundred miles that had a bed open, and he was able to apply for one of the grants they offer.

"Harmony."

"I'm here because I stabbed my stepfather. How about you?" She takes so long to answer I assume she's going to ignore my question. Then she speaks softly, and I instantly like her.

"You're not very bright. Nobody shares why they're here, usually. I guess I'll have to teach you the ropes. Since you're dumb, I'll tell you. I have anorexia. That means I don't like to eat. They'll probably ask you to watch me and tell them if I don't eat. That's what they did to my last roommate."

"How long have you been here?"

"Nine months, you're my third roommate."

"They might ask you stuff about me too. I'm sorry if they do."

"I won't tell them shit." I know at that moment she's going to be my best friend.

"Me neither," I smiled at her. So far, I don't want to stab her, so that's a good sign. She smiles back.

"How old are you?"

"Twelve, you?"

"Fifteen. You're tall for twelve. I thought you were at least fifteen too."

"I get that a lot. What are we allowed to do here?"

"Nothing fun. But I'll show you how to get make-up and candy. Colby can hack into your records. Mike has a contraband connection. Plus, I can teach you which staff can be manipulated and who doesn't care. Nurse Tiffany will give you her speech with all the rules. She's a hateful bitch. Just smile and nod, and don't let her catch you if you break the rules."

"Are we allowed to leave our room?"

"Yeah, you can go to the day room or the library anytime between 8 in the morning and 8 at night. The day room has snacks and we're allowed to watch movies and cavort with the boys. We can only go in their boy hallway before dinner and all doors must remain open if you're in a room other than your own. After it gets late, we have to stay in our room and lights out is at ten."

"Oh, a library! Is it nice?"

"It's okay, the young adult section isn't as big as it should be. There're tons of kid's books. You might be able to have your doctor give you permission to go to the adult library. A kid who used to be down the hall was allowed to go there for one hour a day. He said it was way better than ours. My doctor is an asshole and won't give me permission."

"I'll ask my doctor when I see him."

A nurse walks into our room and looks me over. Harmony rolls her eyes and makes a face which tells me this is the infamous Nurse Tiffany. She's short and thick, her dark hair is pulled tightly into a bun at the base of her neck. She's probably mean because her bun is giving her a headache.

"I'm going to get some lunch. See you, Violet."

"See you, Harmony."

"I'm Nurse Tiffany. This is my unit, and we have rules which must be followed. If you break the rules, you will lose privileges. There will be no fighting or bullying other patients. You will follow the lights out and room restrictions. You will be in the cafeteria at 8 a.m. for breakfast each morning, noon for lunch, and 5:30 p.m. for dinner, otherwise the cafeteria is closed. Snacks are provided in the day room. You may request specific snacks in writing at 8 a.m. Monday morning and you will receive them in your cubby by 2:00 p.m. You will remain in your room from 8 p.m. until 8 a.m. without exception. You will not use the phone unless you have my express permission. You will take your medication without argument. You will bathe no less than every other day. Your hair is a problem. You will keep it groomed, or I will cut it off. You are allowed only the hair tie you have on now, you won't get another, so don't lose it. You will not..." I zoned out at this point. Harmony wasn't kidding this lady is a bitch.

"Do you understand these rules?"

"Yes ma'am," I smile and nod.

This is gonna suck. But I have to believe this is better than jail.

I've been in the psych ward for six months, and now I finally have my day in court. Krewe was able to get my charges reduced to manslaughter with extenuating circumstances. I'm having something called a bench trial. It means a judge will hear the case and make the rulings instead of a jury. In my case, Krewe thought a judge would be more sympathetic. Despite the abuse, the jury may not appreciate what led up to me helping the Beast get to hell. Apparently, a jury may be more affected by the bloody gore of the crime scene, making them turn against me. Krewe also said that women on the jury may be jealous of my looks, again making them unsympathetic. I think that's ridiculous, but he says it's common. So, today begins my bench trial. I'm wearing a dress that is too young for my now thirteen-year-old, womanly body. But Krewe says it's important to remind the judge that I am, in fact, a child.

When we arrive at the courthouse, my guard has me in handcuffs, not even Dr. Nercy could prevent it during transport. He removes them when I'm seated at the defense table. There're a few people around the judge's tall desk. There're two court officers. I think they're called bailiffs. My guard sits on the benches behind me. I have a social worker now too. Her name is Mrs. Gonzalez. She's really sweet but a little out of the loop. She sits beside my guard.

The bailiff yells out, "All rise!" It's just like on TV. The judge comes out from a door behind his desk and sits down. Then everyone else can sit. I look at him and instantly my stomach falls, the room shifts, and I feel sick. The judge is one of the Beasts' friends. I'm having flashbacks of things he's done to me. I begin to shake, dizziness overtakes me, and vomit swirls up my throat.

Krewe looks at my trembling hand, then he looks at my face.

"Violet, what's wrong? You're white as a ghost!"

"The judge...oh God, I'm going to be sick!" I lean over the side of the table and my breakfast splatters on the floor. A bailiff comes running, grabs a trash can, and hands it to me. I turn in my seat and hold it under my face. The bailiff starts yelling into his radio. I vomit again into the trash can. Krewe rubs my back and holds my hair.

"Violet, what's going on?"

My voice is a shaky whisper, as I croak, "The judge is one of the Beast's friends. He's done things to me. I feel like I'm dying. Please Krewe, I have to get out of here, now!"

"Fuck! Hang on, don't look at him. I'll take care of it, okay?" I nod and vomit again.

Krewe stands up, "Your honor, my client has become ill. I need to request a continuance. She needs emergency medical attention."

The judge is pale. His hand trembles violently as he hits the wood with his gavel. I know Krewe told me not to look at him, but I need to make sure he doesn't come near me.

"Granted Mr. Krowley. Court is adjourned until it can be rescheduled," he stands and flees the court room.

Krewe and my guard each hold an arm and lead me to the front entrance of the courthouse. An ambulance pulls up and they guide me to the back door. Krewe rides back to the hospital with me and we go to the ER.

"Violet, I'm so sorry. I don't even know what to say. I'm going to make some calls. We need to get him off the bench and into jail. I'm going to contact the FBI. I can't trust the local police at this point. Holy shit, I can't believe this. I'm calling Dr. Nercy first, he'll meet us here, in the ER. Are you okay?"

My heart is pounding, and I can't inhale a full breath, I still feel dizzy and nauseated. I'm hooked up to a blood pressure cuff and an IV. My guard had to drive his car back to the hospital. I'm glad he's not here, especially if we can't trust the police. He's nice, but I haven't talked to him more than necessary because Krewe told me not to. I take some deep breaths and try to calm my heart before it pounds out of my aching chest.

In the ER, Dr. Nercy is furious. He's yelling, not at me or Krewe, just in general. The FBI agent Krewe called will be here soon. Dr. Nercy made my guard stay in the waiting room. I'm still lightheaded and my stomach is cramped and spinning when I move.

"Oh, good, there's the FBI agent I called. Let me grab him. Be right back."

When Krewe leaves, Dr. Nercy speaks softly to me. "Violet, as soon as you're finished talking to the FBI agent, I'll give you something for your stomach. It'll put you to sleep so I have to wait. I'm sorry. I can't believe this! Those police are useless. You tried to tell them about everyone involved and they wouldn't listen. This should never have happened. My God, how many illegal things has this judge done? Do you need anything? Want some water?"

I nod. It may be childish, but I want a story to distract me. I wonder if he'll tell me one if I ask. May as well try, he and Krewe are the only adults I trust completely. They've each shown me time and again that they care about my well-being, and they want absolutely nothing from me in return.

"Dr. Nercy, may I ask you for a story?" I begin to cry.

"What kind of story?"

"Something with princesses who live happily ever after." He calms himself and gives me a sad look before he sits in a chair.

With barely a moment's hesitation he clears his throat and begins, "Once upon a time, there was a very smart princess who lived in a very tall tower. Her name was Violet and she had purple hair and a beautiful purple dress..."

I feel lost and afraid. I wish I had a mother who gave a shit about me. Before Dr, Nercy can reach the *happily ever after* part, the FBI agent and Krewe enter the room. I sniffle and try to stop my tears, and Krewe hands me a tissue.

"Hello, Violet. I'm Special Agent Elliott Montgomery. Krewe told me what happened, and I don't want to upset you, but I'm going to have to ask you some uncomfortable questions. How does that sound?"

I nod. "Yeah, fine." I hiccup and snort a weird sound. I would normally be embarrassed. I just don't give a shit anymore. Dr. Nercy examines my face. I nod at him, and he nods back.

"Violet, do you remember how many friends Jerry Raider had?"

"No, it wasn't always the same ones. The judge, he was there at least five times." My lip trembles as I fight off tears.

"Okay, if you had to guess, how many friends did Jerry have? Was it more than ten? Twenty? More?"

"I think I was seven or eight the first time he had a friend there. He had two friends I saw the most. One was called Dave, and the other one was Jimbo. Sometimes there would be one friend and one time there were five. At first the Beast only let them watch what he did to me. Then he started taking pictures. Eventually he let them touch me while he took pictures. I might be able to remember some names if I think about it. I've spent a long time trying to block it out. It all came rushing back today," I sob. Dr. Nercy hands me a cup of water, and I smile at him.

"Okay, let's talk about something different. Where did these visits take place?"

"The Beast's office has a secret door and there's a big room behind it. He always called it The Playhouse. There's a bed in there with cuffs, and there're hooks in the ceiling. He had cameras for photos and video cameras. There were a lot of things he used to hurt me, and chairs where everyone could sit to watch. I should've burned it down."

"Did you tell the police about this room?"

"Yes, and my mother told them I was lying. They didn't find any of it, so they didn't believe me."

"Jesus Christ! Who are these police that can't do their damn jobs?" Dr. Nercy's voice is raised as he gets up and stalks across the room. Krewe sits next to me and gives me a reassuring look and another tissue. I smile through my tears with thanks.

"Do you think you could describe these men to a sketch artist?"

I shrug, "I guess I can try."

"Okay, I'll get one here tomorrow. I'll be here with you, Krewe, and Dr. Nercy. You're safe Violet; we'll protect you. You won't have to go back to court with Judge Kramer. Do you have any questions for me?"

"Will I be going back to the psycho-I mean the center?"

Dr. Nercy walks back over to me, "I think it's the safest place for you. Nobody can get in there without authorization. I'm going to block Officer Blake from entering for now, his lack of a gun in the center doesn't make him safe. We can't trust anyone in the police department until this judge situation is resolved. Are you okay with going back there?"

"Yeah, it's familiar. Thank you, all of you. I felt like I was going to die in the court room. Thank you for getting me out, Krewe."

"Of course, hang in there, kiddo. Call one of us if you need anything. Dr. Nercy will make certain you have access to the phone whenever you need it," He looks to Dr. Nercy, who nods.

CHAPTER Six

It's been a few days since the courthouse incident. I spent a day with the sketch artist, and he was able to draw eight different men, including Dave and Jimbo. Agent Montgomery is working on identifying them. He's also gotten a search warrant for Mother's house. Judge Kramer's been arrested and it's a big scandal. It's all over the news. Thankfully, since I'm a minor, they can't put my name out in public, even though I'm emancipated. The court records have to remain sealed, so nobody knows I'm the 'minor victim'.

There's also an internal affairs investigation into the police department to figure out how they blew my case so badly. Apparently, the state attorney is also in trouble and being investigated;

my trial is postponed indefinitely. I'm in protective custody in the psych ward. What a huge mess.

"Violet! Have you seen the new guy that's bunking with Colby?" Harmony asks me.

"No, why?"

"Holy shit, Vi, he's so hot! Do I look okay? Should I put on some makeup?"

"Harmony, you look great, you don't need anything on your face you'll just get in trouble for having it. But you should change out of your sweats. If Nurse Hitler catches you with that stuff you're going to get locked down."

"Oh fuck, duh! Thanks Vi. I'm not worried about Baby Hitler, she's mean, but she's stupid. You gotta go check him out. Didn't Colby ask you to let him borrow that art book?"

I chuckle at her, she's a trip. "It's The Art of War, *not* an art book, goofy!"

"Whatever, go take it to his room so you can see the new guy. You're gonna melt!"

"He can probably hear you. You're practically shouting," she rolls her eyes at me. "Fine. I'll go take him the book."

I grab it from the desk and carry it down the hall. Colby is a nerd like me, he loves video games and reading. He's tall, like over six feet kind of tall. He has reddish blonde hair, pale skin and acne. He's so sweet, and we became friends the minute we met.

He's fifteen and he doesn't treat me like I'm thirteen. I knock on Colby's door even though it's open.

I stick my head in and call out, "Colby? You here?"

"Yeah, come in Violet."

"I brought the book you wanted."

"Awesome! Thanks."

A throat clears from the bed by the window. I look that way and Harmony's right. He's a mighty fine specimen of a man. He has muscles stretching his shirt tight across his chest and upper arms. He has dark, shiny black hair shaved into a fauxhawk. He has a tattoo on the side of his head where it's shaved, and a hole in his lip, eyebrow, and ears. We aren't allowed any jewelry. His eyes lazily slide from my eyes to my lips, then they stutter on my chest before finishing their trek at my feet.

"Oh, right, Violet, this is Max. Max, Violet."

I lift my chin at him, "Hey."

"Hello, Violet. Colby has told me a lot about you, but obviously not enough. How long have you been here?"

"Around six months." He's really nice to look at, but he probably won't like me when he finds out I'm thirteen.

"Hey guys! What's up?" Harmony arrives with some hot pink lipstick and a cute outfit I haven't seen before.

Colby smirks at her, "Harmony, this is Max, my new roommate." Max checks her out, lingering on her legs. He gives her a panty-dropping smile.

"Nice to meet you, Harmony. Colby didn't tell me he knew so many hot girls." Harmony giggles like a cheerleader after too much beer, just like the one in the stupid movie we watched the other day. Max smirks at her, I roll my eyes at both of them.

"I'll see you guys later." I walk towards the door.

Max asks, "Where are you going?"

"I'm going to get some food and read for a while. I'll see you guys later."

"See ya, Vi!" Colby says without looking up.

"Later babes." Harmony adds.

"Bye, Violet." Max tacks on. I give them a lame wave and take off.

When I get back to my room Dr. Nercy is standing there. He hears me enter and turns towards me. "Violet, good, I was just going to look for you. How are you today?"

"I'm okay. What's up?"

"Let's sit." He has a seat and points for me to join him. I sit on the edge of my bed. He takes a calming breath. *Uh oh...* this can't be good.

"Krewe called me with some news. The new judge on your case, Florence Remington's made some rulings. She's throwing out all the charges against you without prejudice. That means the state attorney can refile if they decide they have cause. Krewe thinks they're going to wait until all the investigations are complete, and the dust settles, before they decide. So that leaves us, or you, in limbo. You don't need to be here for medical reasons anymore, so I can release you. However, that'll put you in foster care, and your emancipation is in question. Also, your mother relinquished her parental rights, so you're no longer covered by health insurance. You're on the state Medicaid insurance. Originally, she was ordered to cover you for six months, but that's expired now. I'm getting pressure to release you, but I don't want to abandon you to foster care alone. I want to know what you want to do. I know that's unusual, but Violet, you're very special and I don't want to see you get lost in the foster system. I also don't want anything to happen that'll further traumatize you. I can keep you here, but I would have to fudge your records, to say it's medically necessary. What do you think?"

"Um, wow, I'm not sure. I would like to leave and have my freedom, although it's fairly safe here and I know what to expect. I think I want to be released. You and Krewe have been amazing, and I'll still talk to you. Plus, I may end up back here if I get new charges or they decide to refile. I don't know how to thank you for helping me, and for believing in me. But I'm ready to face the future, whatever it looks like."

He smiles at me. "I had a feeling you'd say that. I have your release paperwork ready to go. I have a plan that I'd like to run by you, too. I spoke with a friend of mine and he and his wife are taking the foster parent training course. They're approved as a temporary foster placement for thirty days. They'll be done and approved for permanent foster placement by the end of the thirty days. They want to take you. Will you meet them?" I'm truly stunned. Both Dr. Nercy and Krewe have gone above and beyond to help me. I don't even know what to say. It sounds amazing.

"Yeah, I'd love to meet them. I'll never be able to repay you for everything you've done for me... it means a lot. I've never had any adults I could rely on. You and Krewe have given me renewed faith in humanity. I needed that as much as a roof over my head. Thank you. When can I meet them?"

"I'm setting it up for tomorrow. Krewe will join us so we can make certain we have any legal issues addressed. I've assured them that you aren't violent. Please don't scare them, okay?"

I laugh. "I won't scare them on purpose. I promise. Will you tell me about them?"

"I went to college with Xander Henley. He was my roommate for four years. We've been friends ever since. I went to medical school, and he went to work as a financial advisor. He met Emerson when he went to work at Franklin-Madison. They got married after about a year. They've been unable to have children and decided to foster and possibly adopt. They're fairly well off and have a nice home with plenty of room for a thirteen-year-old."

"They sound kind of amazing. Do you think they'll like me?"

"How could they not? You're smart, funny, and kind, if you overlook your tendency to stab certain people," he chuckles at my fake annoyed face.

"I think I'm nervous. What should I wear to meet them?"

"Violet, they won't care how you're dressed. Just be you, they won't be able to resist your wit. I'll continue to see you for therapy. Krewe will still be your attorney. We're just adding to the people who care about you. I've no doubt they'll like you. I like you, and I don't like anybody," he jokes.

"Yes, you do. You like Krewe, and now I find out you have another friend. You might be nicer than you let on." I gave him a big grin.

I know he's my doctor, but sometimes I feel like he's a big brother or my favorite uncle. He's done so much for me, and most of all he's respected my needs and my thoughts. I don't know how I went from horribly mistreated by every adult I encountered, to finding my heroes.

Harmony comes into our room. She looks Dr. Nercy over, and I can tell she thinks he's handsome. I've learned she thinks every male is attractive in some way. She gives him her best flirty smile. He skillfully ignores her efforts in a very polite but professional way.

"Hi, Dr. Nercy," she purrs at him.

"Hello, Harmony. Okay Violet, I'll see you about 11 tomorrow morning. Have a good day, ladies." He salutes us and exits.

Harmony hugs herself. "He's so dreamy, don't you think? Oh! And how about Max? So yummy!"

I can't help laughing at her, she's beyond boy crazy. It's pretty entertaining. But despite her boy crazy antics, I love her. I've never had a girlfriend before, and she's a good one.

"I'm leaving soon. I'm going to move to a foster home. Some foster parents are coming to meet me tomorrow." She frowns at me.

"I'm going to keep in touch with you Harmony. I've never had a friend like you. I'm not gonna let you get away. We can visit once you're out."

"Okay. It sucks because I'll miss you. You're my ride or die friend. But, if you're gone, I'll have Max all to myself. The boys always like you better than me, because you're so pretty, and they don't know how stabby you can be." We crack up, she's my ride or die too. I love her and I truly won't ever let her get away.

CHAPTER SEVEN

"Hi, it's so nice to meet you, Mr. and Mrs. Henley." The people Dr. Nercy had set up for me were just as he described. They were kind, rich, and eager to have a kid, even if it was my stabby self.

"Violet, please, call me Emmy and you can call him Xander. No need for formality with us."

"Thank you, Emmy. What would you like to know about me?" I look between her and Xander. They both smile at me, and I twist my hands around nervously. Krewe and Dr. Nercy are smiling at me too. I hate being the center of attention.

"What type of things do you like to do?"

"I love to read, it's my favorite thing. I like all types of books. I like to learn new things. I love food, but I don't know how to cook. I'd love to learn some type of martial arts. I don't get enough exercise here. I like music a lot but again, I don't get much chance to listen to it here. I think I'd like to do things outside, like hiking and camping. But I've never done either. I don't know how to ride a bicycle or swim. Those are things I can't learn from a book. I'm good on the computer and I love to explore online and play games. Minecraft is really fun. I hate social media though."

"You're in luck. We love hiking, biking, and camping. Do you like dogs?" Xander asks.

Emmy takes over, "We have a yellow lab, Copper. He's a sweetie. I also like MMA, which is mixed martial arts. I'd love to work with you."

They seem either very excited or very nervous, maybe it's both. We spend at least an hour getting to know one another. They'll be taking me to their home on Friday. I'm excited and nervous too.

After they leave Harmony finds me. "Well? How did it go with the fosters?"

"Their names are Emmy and Xander Henley. Oh, and they have a dog, Copper. They're super nice. I'm excited but I'm trying not to get too excited. They might not like me when they know me better. What if they return me?"

"Pshaw!" Harmony scoffs at me.

"Why would they return you? You'll be their favorite human in no time. Look how fast you grew on me, and I hate everyone who doesn't have a dick. Just let them see the sweet you, not the stabby you. You're not having the nightmares anymore, so that won't scare them off. I think you've got this in the bag. Fuck! I'm gonna miss your giant ass!"

"What did I tell you? I'm not a giant, you're just a pixie. I think you might be smaller than Tinker Bell. Although, you're doing well on your new diet. I think you're looking very healthy."

"Thanks, *mom*. I'll really miss you. You had better call me every week and come visit me at least once a month once I'm free. Here, pinky swear."

She holds her little finger out to me. I wrap mine around hers and promise. Her doctor told her if she gains five more pounds, she'll be able to go home. Every time she gets close, she sabotages herself and starts losing again. She swears she's not trying to avoid something at home, but what else could it be? I hope my leaving doesn't trigger weight loss for her. She's really looking so much better.

There's a knock on our door. Harmony closed it when she came in and Dr. Nercy did the same when he left. She pulls the heavy door open.

"Hey Max, what's up?"

"Hi Harmony, there's a rumor circulating that you're leaving, Violet. Is it true?" He peeks over her head at me.

"That was quick. Yeah, I'm leaving on Friday. I'm going to a foster placement. Are you gonna miss me, Max?"

"Yeah of course. You two are the most interesting chicks here. If you're gone, Harmony is going to end up with all of my attention. Can you handle that, Harmony?"

She flutters her lashes at him. "That doesn't sound bad at all Max." she giggles. I roll my eyes.

"I bet you say that to all the girls here!" I add.

He grabs his chest. "You wound me! You ladies are my sole focus. I'd never look at another girl." He flashes his charming smile. I shake my head at his antics.

His brown eyes narrow at me. "Can we have a going away party?"

"You actually think Nurse Tiffany would let us have a party? Please! She'd rather lock us in our rooms and throw away the key." The hateful bitch. Harmony nailed that description. Nurse Tiffany Hitler has a nose for happiness. She seeks it out and stomps on it every chance she gets.

"I have my ways. Meet us in the cafeteria tonight at 7:45, yeah?"

"Who's us?" Harmony asks.

"Me, Colby, and Mike."

Her face lights up, "Okay. We'll be there. Should we bring any-thing?"

"Nah, we got it covered. See you lovely ladies later."

I'm about to speak out against this very bad idea, but Harmony puts her hand over my mouth. "Mm hmmm, mm tay..."

"Yeah, we'll see you later. Thanks, Max!"

At 7:45 p.m. sharp, Harmony and I tiptoe into the cafeteria. At first, I don't see the boys, but they're in the corner by the door to the kitchen. Harmony is about to shout out to them. I grab her arm and shush her. Thankfully we walk quietly over to the boys. Mike is tall, and bulky like a football player, with dark hair and eyes. He has a killer smile, but he's extremely shy. The most he's ever said to me was hello.

"What's the plan Max?" I whisper.

"Follow us, but be super quiet, Harmony that means you." He smirks at her.

Max takes the lead, and we all follow, Mike takes the rear with Harmony, me, and Colby in the middle. He pushes through the kitchen door and goes to the rear mud room. He turns right and goes up the stairs. I've never been this way before, it's in a *staff only* area. Max has only been here a short time. I'm surprised he knows to go this way.

When we reach the top of the stairs there's a door that says, *Roof Access Only, Keep Door Locked*. He opens the door, and it creaks softly. Hopefully nobody can hear it. He holds the door for all of us to file through. I watch as he puts a wedge of wood under the door propping it open just a crack. The roof is strictly off limits to everyone but the staff, so nobody can jump.

Then he leads us to the far end of the roof. There's a gazebo, and outdoor furniture underneath it. An L shaped sofa, coffee table, and two chairs sit opposite. It's nice up here. There're even some potted plants adding to the atmosphere. I like it and I smile at Max.

"This is nice. I had no idea this was up here. How did you know?"

"I confess, I may know a guy who was here before me. He may have told me a few secrets, like who to bribe and who doesn't give a shit. You like?"

"I do. I wish I knew sooner. This is a great place to get away and read." He pulls a joint out of his pocket with a lighter.

"That's not all it's good for..." he strikes the lighter and the flame comes to life. His face glows in the orange light as he touches it to the end of the rolled paper. He smiles and passes it to Colby who takes a big inhale and holds it in. He hands it to Harmony who takes a drag and holds it in as well. She hands it to me. I've never tried it before. What the hell, I'm leaving the day after tomorrow. You only live once, right?

I pinch it in my fingers and suck in some smoke, then I cough it right back out. My eyes water as I cough. I try again, this time taking a much smaller puff and holding it in. I hand it off to Mike. He takes a huge inhale and holds it in, passing it back to Max. He looks experienced like Max. Actually, everyone did okay except for me. I'm the youngest here and obviously the least experienced.

We continue to pass it until it's gone. It smells terrible like a skunk, but my vision is a bit wavy, and I feel a warm tingle spreading through my body. My face is hot and I kinda like it.

We're spread out on the furniture and chatting quietly when Mike starts talking, and I'm shocked since he never says anything. Maybe pot is the key to his voice. He's animated as he tells us about his friends at school. He's really funny. We all crack up over and over again.

Colby pulls a bottle out of his pants, and I have to know, "How did you get that?"

"My doctor falls asleep while I talk, he keeps alcohol in his desk. I think it's why he falls asleep," Colby explains.

It's vodka according to the label. He unscrews the cap and takes a gulp. He passes it to Max, and we continue to share it around just like the pot. I guess if you're rich and your parents don't want you around you learn how to make this place a little more tolerable. I can't really blame the staff for being so bribe-able, they don't make squat and the kids in here are loaded. Except for me. But I hit the jackpot with friends. Plus, living in a place where the adults aren't molesting me is a big improvement. I hope I like it at the Henleys.

I don't want much vodka, I'm happy with my marijuana buzz. I was forced to drink whiskey a few times in my traumatic past and I don't like it. I take a small sip on the first pass and decline after that.

"You don't want to drink, Violet?" Max asks me.

"Nah, I had a bad experience with whiskey in the past. I don't like it, but you guys go ahead."

Harmony says, "I love vodka, I'll drink hers!" She bursts out laughing. I'm not sure what's funny, but she's silly and I laugh at her.

They share it around a few more times, then Colby puts the lid back on. He sets it on the coffee table. Max, Harmony, and Colby are sitting on the couch. Mike and I are sitting in the chairs.

"Should we be worried about being out of our rooms for so long? Won't someone come looking for us?" I ask nervously.

"Don't worry, babe. It's under control. The staff is playing poker with the money I used to bribe them. Nobody's looking for us. Relax." Max soothes.

Harmony gets a mischievous look on her face. "I've got an idea! Let's play a game!"

"You're so loud Harmony," I whisper yell at her.

"Come on Vi, let's play spin the bottle."

"Yes! I'll go first." Max grabs the bottle and lays it on its side. He spins it. The neck spins around and it settles to a stop pointing at Mike. He gets up off the couch and walks to Mike. He bends down and kisses Mike on the lips. Mike looks surprised, but not unhappy. The dark skin of his cheeks turns pink. Max sits back in his seat and Mike leans forward to spin. He lands on Harmony, and she squeals in delight. We chuckle at her, she's pretty wasted.

Mike gets up and Harmony hops off the couch. She jumps on him climbing him, like a monkey on a tree. Her arms wrap around his neck and her legs wrap around his waist. I'm thankful she's wearing leggings and not a skirt. She purrs and moans as she kisses him. I think I see tongue. Holy crap! When she's done, he sets her down and she stumbles back to her seat. Mike is really red now. When he sits down, he puts his hands in his lap attempting to hide the tent there.

Harmony spins the bottle, and it lands on Colby. He gets a huge grin on his face and Max smirks at him. I'm pretty sure Colby has a crush on Harmony. She climbs on his lap straddling him. She kisses him fiercely, and again with tongue, both of them making a groaning sound. She climbs off him and wipes her mouth as she settles back into her seat, a wide grin on her face. He also tries to cover his lap. Colby spins the bottle next, and it stops on me. He stands and sways on his feet. I decide to help him out. I walk over and meet him where he sways. I lean in and kiss him on the lips, no tongue. I squeeze his shoulder and smile at him before I return to my seat. His cheeks are pink, and mine are probably glowing red. He falls into his spot on the sofa and he's still attempting to hide his lap. I lean over and spin. It points to Max when its momentum stops. He hops out of his seat before I can move. He takes my hand and pulls me up. He wraps his arms around me and softly places a chaste kiss on my lips. I hug him back and give him a grateful smile.

We play round after round until everyone has kissed everyone. Harmony is plastered and having the time of her life. I'm tired and ready for my bed. I'm glad we did this, and I realize I have four friends, not just one. I'll do my best to keep in touch with them. When we sneak back inside, we'll have to work to keep Harmony from getting us noticed. Thankfully Nurse Tiffany isn't here at night, and we successfully make it back to our rooms without getting caught or maybe the bribes kept us in the clear. I have to spend an extra half hour getting Harmony to stay in her bed. When she finally passes out, I'm so thankful. I think I fell asleep the second my head hit the pillow.

When Friday arrives, I'm packed and ready to start my new adventure. I've said my goodbyes. Dr. Nercy has released me, and my social worker has approved my placement with the Henleys. It seems for once in my life things are going right.

CHAPTER Eight

The Henley's have a fancy, Porsche SUV. The leather is so soft, I keep rubbing my fingers across the back seat. They chat with me on the way to my new home. They tell me about their house, my room, and what to expect rule wise. Basically, we're going to play it by ear on the rules. I'll have bedtime at first, and no adult sites on the computer, everything's very reasonable.

School is a different issue. I had a tutor once a week in the hospital, now, I can actually attend school. I have a choice between a private high school or a public high school. Based on my test scores, I'm at an 11th grade level in high school. My age would put me in 8th grade. I can also choose home school, but they don't want me to do that. They really want me to have a normal school experience, as much as possible. But between my placement scores and my history, they agree I may have a hard time no matter what. We're going to discuss it more with Dr. Nercy. He's coming for dinner tomorrow night. Apparently, I also have a foster grandmother, she's coming for dinner too. It's a lot but I'm using my coping tools and so far, no panic or anxiety attacks. Violet for the win!

When we can see the house, they point it out. My room will be upstairs. Emmy had a lot of fun decorating it in purple, my favorite color. I even have an ensuite bathroom. The house looks huge to me. They told me it wasn't all that big, but it has five bedrooms and three and a half bathrooms. They also have an in-home gym and a swimming pool. They already hired a swimming teacher for me.

The house sits on an acre and a half. The whole property is enclosed with a wall. We pass through a gate as we drive up the stone-paved circle. There are big oak trees scattered across the front lawn draped with moss, it's pretty. The style of the house looks Spanish or maybe Italian. It has clay barrel tiles on the roof and wrought iron scroll work around the windows, and the double front doors are arched at the top. I haven't seen anything like it before.

Emmy is bouncing on her toes as she's so excited to show me around. She's a beautiful woman, petite, with long blonde hair. She has brown eyes, but they aren't dark like mine. Xander is so tall, Emmy only reaches his arm pit. He has dark hair and blue eyes. He's nice looking in an executive sort of way. They both have beautiful bright white teeth and they're quick to smile. I can't wait to visit their dentist. He must have magic powers to get teeth that white.

Xander carries my suitcase and Emmy opens the door to let us inside. Normally they would pull into the four-car garage, but they wanted me to enter from the front for the first time. There are gleaming wood floors and tasteful art in the foyer, and a stunning chandelier hangs overhead.

"Wow! This is amazing! What a beautiful house."

Emmy smiles at me, "Let's start with your room. Xander can bring your bag upstairs and I can show you the things I picked out for you. I bought a few casual clothes, and some pajamas. I'll take you shopping for clothes once you're settled. Don't feel obligated to wear what I picked out. Same with your room, anything you don't like we can change." Emmy beams at me.

"I'm sure everything's very nice. Thank you so much."

She leads me upstairs and Xander follows us. There're two rooms upstairs, one is my bedroom with the ensuite bath, the other is a den they've made into an office for me to study, read, or do computer stuff. My ensuite is actually a Jack and Jill bathroom that joins my room and the office. The entire upstairs is mine. I'm completely blown away. I wasn't expecting this.

She throws open the bedroom door and steps aside for me to enter. There's a king-sized bed draped in violet. It has a thick comforter and about a dozen pillows. There's white furniture, a long dresser with a mirror and a tall dresser. There's a light purple velvet loveseat in the corner. It's breathtaking, I love it. I was really worried it would be juvenile and inappropriate for a teen, but it's perfect. My eyes actually fill with happy tears.

"Oh God, Violet, are you okay? Really anything you don't like, we can change. I'm sorry!"

"No, Emmy, I love it! It's beautiful. Thank you so much!" I grab her in a tight hug. I'm usually not one for physical affection, but I'm overwhelmed with emotion, and I don't know how else to express it. She wipes tears from her eyes.

Xander smiles at her, "Told you she'd like it."

"I do! It's so nice, I don't even know what to say. Thank you both so much."

Wiping her eyes Emmy releases me, "I'm so glad sweetie. Xander please set her suitcase in the closet. You can unpack later."

"Check out the bathroom, she did that in purple too." Xander nods in the direction of the ensuite.

I open the bathroom door and it's huge. It has a very large walk-in shower and a soaking tub. There's a little closet where the toilet is and there's a huge cabinet with a long granite countertop and two sinks. It's all done in gray and purple, it's gorgeous. The towels are a variety of grape and lilac. The purple goes perfectly with the shade of gray on the tiles, granite, and walls.

"I think I'm out of adjectives to express how beautiful this is, everything's amazing and I love it. Thank you so much for doing all of this."

"Of course, dear, it really was fun for me. I really like the purple. Let's go check out your office." Emmy leads the way out of the room.

"My office. That sounds surreal." I smile at her and Xander and they smile back. Soon, we're all smiling like idiots. But I feel a happy hum in my chest. This is so unimaginably amazing. I need to pinch myself to make sure it's real.

My office is wall to wall white bookshelves. There's a window seat built in under the big window, it's light and bright. The walls are a light lilac with white trim. There are sheer mauve curtains, a white desk sits near the window, with a laptop computer installed, and two extra screens. They set it up with me in mind. There's a printer, not that people use them much anymore, but I'll likely need it for school. The bookshelves are half full, with plenty of space to add more books. I see some classics and some reference books.

"It's wonderful! Absolutely perfect. Again, I don't know what to say."

"I'm so glad sweetie. No need to say anything. We're so happy you like it."

"Let's head downstairs ladies. We still need to show her everything in the rest of the house and Copper is probably dying to meet her," Xander says.

"Oh yeah, poor Copper. We closed him in the study so he wouldn't jump all over you the minute you walked in the door. Yeah, we better get down there."

We follow Xander down the stairs. He points out the living room, kitchen, and dining room. We pass a half bath and when he opens the next door, a large gold colored dog comes running out. His tail is wagging like crazy. He runs up to me and sniffs me. I squat down and hold out my hand for him to sniff and he licks it. Then he licks my cheek, I giggle. I scratch behind his ear, and he presses against me. He's adorable and so sweet.

"Oh, he likes you! That's great, he's usually friendly but sometimes he doesn't like certain people. I'm so glad he likes you." I laugh as he licks my arm while I scratch him. We're going to be good friends, I can tell.

Emmy fixes us lunch and we sit at the breakfast table to eat our sandwiches. I like it here, it feels comfortable. When we're done, I go upstairs to unpack. They give me some space to settle in and put my things away.

Dr. Nercy just arrived for our dinner. I fling the door open before he can even knock. I might be excited. It's good to see him outside of the hospital. Harmony isn't wrong, he is nice looking. But to me he's just Dr. Nercy, my friend, my therapist, my hero. I can't help but think of him as family, I wonder how he feels about me. I'll probably never know, and that's okay. I'm happy he's in my life, since he's helped me more than anyone else ever has in my thirteen years.

This is the first time I've seen him without a doctor's white coat on. He has dark gray slacks and a pale blue button up shirt that has the sleeves rolled up and I can see a tattoo. Interesting.

His face breaks into a warm smile, "Violet, how're you doing?"

I return his smile, "I'm good. My room is awesome, it's purple, my favorite, and I have my own office. It's got a computer and endless bookshelves. I can't wait to read all the books. Emmy and Xander are great, I really like them. Oh, and I just adore Copper. He slept in my bed last night." I couldn't help but tell him everything. I was just too excited.

"Wow! I guess things are going well, you've never spoken so much at one time before," he chuckles. "I'm happy to see you settling in. You deserve some good things in your life, and good people. I knew Xander and Emmy would be a good fit for you." He's smiling so brightly it lights up his face, I've never seen him so animated. I guess this is good for both of us.

I lead him into the living room and have him sit on the sofa. I ask what he would like to drink, and he requests a beer. I go into the kitchen to get it for him. When I remove it from the fridge and use a bottle opener to pop off the cap Xander looks at me with wide eyes and his mouth open.

"Dr. Nercy's here, it's not for me, I swear!"

He laughs and a gush of air leaves him. "Phew! You had me worried for a second."

"I don't like alcohol. I won't willingly have any, I promise." His smile falls from his face realizing the connection to my past.

"Violet, I'm sorry, that was dumb of me," he reaches out to my arm then stops short. I'm certain he was advised not to initiate physical contact with me. Poor guy, he's trying so hard.

I decide to offer him a bone, "No worries Xander. We can talk about everything. I want you guys to feel comfortable talking to me about anything." I reach out to him and pat his arm.

"You know Violet, sometimes it's difficult to remember that you're only thirteen. You're very wise and observant, thank you for being understanding. I think we're going to do just fine," he gives me a kind smile and I return it.

"I think so too, Xander." I head into the living room and hand Dr. Nercy his beer. Emmy has joined him, and they quickly stop talking when I walk into the room.

"Randy and I were just talking about you. I was telling him how much you like your room and how well you slept last night." She smiles and I appreciate her honesty. She's a lovely person, so kind and considerate. She also has great taste. She's taking me clothes shopping this weekend, and I'm excited about it. A knock sounds at the door, and I can hear Xander answer it.

He shows an older woman into the living room. She's little, maybe hovering at just over five feet tall. Her hair is short and streaked gray. She's wearing a very expensive looking pantsuit, it's red and makes her pale blue eyes stand out. Her wrinkles make her look like she wears a permanent frown. Her mouth is just a slash outlined in red lipstick with eyebrows that look drawn on and they're comically high on her forehead. Her wrists are dripping with gold and her ears sparkle with diamond studs. She looks wealthy, but in a trying too hard sort of way. I tilt my head as I inspect her.

"Xander, go get me a scotch like a good son-in-law, neat."

Emmy jumps up from the sofa. "Mom, I'm so glad you're here. Let me introduce you."

"Violet, this is my mother, Joyce Morgan. Mom, this is Violet. I know I've told you all about her, but isn't she beautiful?" She narrows her eyes at me and scans me from head to toe.

Her lips pucker and her nose scrunches into a look of disapproval, "Yes, beautiful, from what you said, experienced too. Are you sure you can trust your husband with a pretty young thing in the house?"

Xander and Dr. Nercy both snap their heads to Joyce. Dirty looks of shock cover their faces. I can see Xander is fighting not to snap at her horrific comment.

"Mom! Don't be ridiculous. Please apologize to Xander and Violet. That was incredibly rude."

"I suppose. Sorry."

She sashays across the room and seats herself in the armchair next to the fireplace. She acts like the Queen, sitting upon her throne as she looks down at the rest of us. Boy, she's a real piece of work. I paste a fake smile on my face and bite my tongue. I don't want to insult Emmy's mom in the first five minutes. Xander excuses himself to make her drink. Poor Emmy is wringing her hands.

Dr. Nercy takes up the reigns, "Hello, Mrs. Morgan, it's so nice to see you again. I trust you're doing well?"

"Oh yes, Rodney, I'm doing very well. I've just had a full medical checkup and I'm healthy as can be. You're a doctor, aren't you?"

"It's Randy, and yes ma'am. I'm a pediatric psychiatrist. I work at Mystic Cross Medical Center, and in their mental health unit."

"Well, that's nice dear. I'm sure you're useful to somebody over there. I'm looking for a good plastic surgeon, now *they're* good doctors. Do you know any of those you could recommend?"

"No, not off the top of my head," he shrugs at Emmy. She grimaces and smiles at him.

"So, Mom, what type of procedure are you thinking about having. I don't think you need any plastic surgery. You look great."

"Of course I do, because I take precautions before going out in the sun. I also have a very strict nighttime moisturizing ritual. You can't look like this without moisturizer. I've told you that since you were a teen, and you never listen. You already need Botox. I'm looking for someone to do some preventative measures before I need a facelift."

I don't even know what to say, I decide to just sit quietly and hope she doesn't insult me again. Xander comes into the room with a glass in each hand. He hands one to Joyce and takes a gulp from the other. I think this woman could drive a saint to drink.

"Violet, you may call me Joyce. I'm too young to be a grandmother and you're not family, so I think that will suffice. Tell me what you're studying in school." Her gaze is penetrating and makes me uncomfortable.

"I, uh, I'm not in school yet, Joyce. We're deciding which school I'll attend. I used to be home schooled, and I've had a tutor the last several months." I slap on a sarcastic wide smile.

"Home school! That's ridiculous. You must be very behind in your studies, tsk tsk tsk." She looks at Emmy like she has personally kept me from school.

"Violet is very bright, Mom. She's only thirteen which would have her in 8th grade, but she tested at an 11th grade level, and college level in some subjects. We're debating what grade she

should enter, and which school would be most beneficial for her."
Emmy lifts her chin in defiance. Dr. Nercy looks proud. I'm not
sure if he's proud of my intelligence or Emmy's fight. I'm proud of
Emmy for standing up for me. It feels good, there's a warm feeling
in my chest, having someone stick up for me is a new experience.

"Which schools are you considering?"

"She can enter the high school or middle school in our district.
Gulf Bay, or she can enter the private school, Bayshore Academy.
They go from sixth through twelfth grade."

"She should go to the public school. You shouldn't have to pay
for private school while you're just foster parents."

"We don't have any issue paying for private school for Violet.
We just want the best fit for her, so she can succeed in her studies."
Again, they stick up for me. Remind me why anyone thought
bringing Joyce here was a good idea...

"I don't see how it's your responsibility to pay for her education.
What if she can't even function in a school? Then you'd really be
wasting your money."

"For us, it's not about the money. We just want whatever's best
for Violet."

Dr. Nercy's practically foaming at the mouth. "Violet's extremely intelligent, and her test scores were excellent. She also did very
well on her personality tests, I see no reason why she wouldn't
excel in any school," he looks to Xander. "How much longer until
dinner's ready? I'm starving."

Xander startles, he's probably trying to block out his mother-in-law. "Oh, um, it should be close, I'll go check on it." Right as he stands, we hear a buzzing noise from the direction of the kitchen.

His face lights up, "There we go. Why don't you all get situated in the dining room?"

Emmy and I sit on one side of the table. Dr. Nercy sits at the far end. Joyce sits on the opposite side from Emmy. That leaves the head of the table for Xander. He must have previously established that spot as his with Joyce, or I'm certain she would've taken his seat.

Xander carries in a large platter with some type of roast on it, surrounded by vegetables. There was already a salad on the table when we sat down. He goes back to the kitchen and returns with two bowls. One contains rolls and the other has green beans. It smells so good my mouth waters.

There's a large knife next to the platter. The blade looks to be about ten inches long and it's serrated. It has two small prongs on the end like a fork. It looks like a great knife for cutting through bone and tendon. I imagine using it to silence Joyce.

Somehow Dr. Nercy can read my mind and clears his throat. When I look at him, he shakes his head no. My eyes go wide. How did he know? I smirk at him. He opens his eyes wide and pinches his lips together, then shakes his head, reinforcing his admonishment. I sigh in acquiescence. I find it intriguing how people who know each other well can communicate without words.

Xander picks up the knife and carves the roast. Dr. Nercy can't stop my mind from seeing Joyce's neck under the blade. I smile with satisfaction. Dinner continues without any more inappropriate comments from Joyce. She talks about where she's going on vacation and as long as all the attention is on her, she's able to be decent to everyone else. After dessert she complains that she's tired. I think about helping her rest, permanently.

Thankfully Joyce left when we cleared away the dishes. The rest of us moved to lounge in the living room. They want to discuss my school options, as it starts in a week. I want to visit the schools and see what they're like before we decide.

"That's a great idea Violet. It's hard to choose when you haven't even seen them. I'll call them both tomorrow and see if we can get a tour."

"Good. I'm ready for bed. This was a long day."

"I'm sorry for my mom's behavior. She gets worse every time I see her. You would never believe I grew up in a lower middle-class home. I don't know how she became such a snob. It's so embarrassing admitting she's, my mother."

"Don't feel bad, Emmy. It's not your fault she acts like that, I don't blame you." I offer her a smile hoping she won't feel so bad.

"Maybe her last husband influenced her behavior. His death made her very wealthy, and he wasn't particularly nice. I met him at your wedding, and he was an ass," Dr. Nercy adds.

"What I don't get is why she cares what we spend our money on. It's not like she's going to get any of it. We've worked hard to get where we are and if we want to pay for Violet to go to private school, that's our choice. I swear she gives me a migraine every time she's here. She wasn't nice to Violet at all, I don't think we should invite her around Violet again." Xander suggests.

"You're right. I keep forgetting my mother has turned into an evil woman." I think Emmy and I have something in common here. My mother was turned into a monster by the Beast, though she was bad even before that. At least I don't feel alone.

"I'm going to head home. Thanks for inviting me. Violet, I'll see you Saturday for our session. Right?"

"Yeah, sounds great. Thanks for coming tonight." We all stand, Dr. Nercy shakes hands with Xander and thanks him. He kisses Emmy on her cheek, and he pats my shoulder. After he's gone, we all head to our rooms for the night.

CHAPTER NINE

After we visited the public and private schools, I decide I like the private school the best. The classes are much smaller, and the elective options are much more interesting. The other reason is they offer a program for juniors and seniors to simultaneously attend college courses. I can graduate high school with an AA degree. All of that's very appealing to me. I also really liked the guidance counselor we met with. She had great suggestions. I especially liked her advice to have me enter in 10th grade, even though I tested for 11th grade. She pointed out it would be a bit less jarring age-wise, and when I graduate, I'll be almost eighteen instead of sixteen going on seventeen. It's not so far out of the norm for me to enter college at seventeen vs. sixteen. I have a good feeling about the private school. I hope I like the other students. They require uniforms, the one negative I've found so far. But Emmy still insists on taking me clothes shopping.

We go to the local mall. I find a few skirts and dresses that Emmy really likes. I prefer jeans and t-shirts, so she gets me five pairs of jeans. I pick out some concert t-shirts in a store aimed at young people. She also has me get some tops that aren't t-shirts but still go with jeans. I really love the purple sparkly shirt she found. It goes great with my hair and eyes.

I want to cut my hair by about eight inches or so. She takes me to the salon in the mall and they're happy to help us. It turns out they're having a Locks of Love hair donation event. I've never heard of this, but it's cool. They accept donations of hair in lengths of ten inches or more and they must be braided or in a ponytail. The hair is then made into hair pieces or wigs for kids who have hair loss, usually from chemotherapy. I met some kids who were bald and having treatment when I was in the hospital. I'd be honored to help a kid this way. Emmy cries when the guy cuts my hair.

"Violet, I'm so proud of you. What a selfless thing to do. If my hair was longer I would do it too," she's beaming at me.

"I met some kids in treatment when I was in the hospital. I would've gladly given them some hair. I had no idea this was even an option. I'm going to grow it longer again and do it again when it's long enough." She hugs me. It surprises me but I hug her back.

When Enrique is finished with my hair, he spins my chair with a flourish. I look in the mirror, it looks great, and I feel so much lighter. It hangs below my shoulders in long waves. He did some layering around my face, and it hangs perfectly.

"I really love it! Thanks so much Enrique."

"No, thank you my dear. This charity is close to my heart. My cousin has lymphoma and she's been bald three times from chemo. So, truly, thank you!" We all smile like lunatics. I follow Emmy to the front desk. Turns out the salon is offering ten dollars towards styling if you donate ten inches to Locks of Love. Win-win!

We had a great time spending the day at the mall. I even got a couple pairs of shoes. I have a whole new wardrobe and then some. Xander brought home some school supplies for me last night, he got me a purple backpack. I'm all set to start school next Monday.

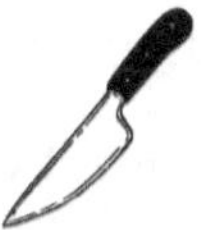

I'm jumpy in my seat as Emmy drives me to the psycho center at the hospital. Dr. Nercy was able to get approval for me to visit, it's usually not allowed. I'm visiting Harmony and I have butterflies in my belly. It's so strange being just a visitor. As I pass through the security doors, it feels wrong. The door closes with an ominous clang behind me.

Harmony comes running and almost tackles me with a hug. I've missed her so much and it's only been a week. She talks a mile a minute asking me so many questions I'll never remember them all to answer. The most interesting bit of news... she's dating Mike. It's probably a match made in heaven since he's so quiet and she never shuts up. I love it.

"I know you probably can't imagine me liking just one guy, but Vi, he's amazing in bed. He's so big, everywhere, I might be in love. Don't tell him that though, I have to keep him guessing so he doesn't lose interest."

"So how excited are you for school to start? Are you nervous? You haven't been to school in so long. Are you worried about mean girls? You know you can't stab anyone right? Oh, my God, I'm so excited for you. You're going to be the mysterious new girl. You'll probably have all the hot guys following you around. What grade are you going to try? High school boys are so much better than middle school boys. Wait until you see how forward they are, they don't play those middle school games. I wish I could go with you. I gained a pound. Only four more to go. So, tell me, how're you doing?"

Laughing, I answer, "I love you, Harmony!"

"Of course you do. Why wouldn't you? I'm lots of fun!" She looks at me with a straight face. I shake my head and try to stop giggling. She is lots of fun.

"I decided to try tenth grade. The guidance counselor suggested it and I agree with her reasons. I start Monday at Bayshore. I'm nervous, but excited. Like sixty percent excited and forty percent nervous. I'm required to wear a uniform, which I don't care for, but it should put everyone on even ground. I'm so proud of you, gaining a pound. That's so great. Keep going, okay?"

"I will, Mike is probably getting out of here in a few weeks. I need to get out too. He wants to keep seeing me on the outside. Dr. Hernandez thinks he's a good influence."

"That's so great, I'm happy for you guys. How's Colby? And Max?"

"I think Colby's coming out to see you." The door opens and Colby and Max walk out to the visitor room. They smile at me.

"Hi Violet. How's it going?" Colby leans in and hugs me.

"Really good. How about you? Hey Max."

"Hi Violet. He's good, he misses you. Nobody else understands his computer jargon." Colby chuckles and his cheeks turn pink.

"He means he's sick of hearing about stuff he doesn't under-stand," he smirks at Max.

I enjoyed my visit with my friends. I can't believe I have friends. I was trapped alone with monsters for so long. It's amazing to feel kinda normal. I hope school goes well next week.

CHAPTER TEN

I survived my first day at school. No mean girls threw their lunch on me. No boys did anything inappropriate. I like most of my teachers. I absolutely love my computer science teacher. He's cool. I think he's a secret hacker. He let me do my own thing, and he's letting us choose our own projects. I'm thinking about searching for some monsters and turning them into the authorities as my project. We have to present our topics for approval Friday. I hope he approves mine.

Emmy's super proud of me. Xander listened intently to every detail of my day. I'm beginning to adjust to having adults who care about me. I've never been happy before, and I really like the feeling.

"Violet, will you take Copper out for me?"

"Sure, come on Copper, let's go outside."

He wags his tail as he follows me out. After he does his business, he brings me a ball. I throw it for him, and he brings it back covered with slobber.

"Yuck! Copper, you gotta learn how to bring it back without your spit, buddy." His tail wags as he tilts his head. I throw it again. We stay outside for half an hour. When we go back in, my social worker, Mrs. Gonzalez, is in the living room with Emmy and Xander. They all look at me when I enter the room.

"Hi, Mrs. Gonzalez, I didn't know you were coming."

"Hello Violet, it's an unannounced visit. I'm required to make them every so often. Mr. and Mrs. Henley were just telling me how you're doing with the start of school. I'd like to speak with you alone if that's okay with you?"

"Yes ma'am. Would you like to see my room?"

"Sure, that sounds great." She follows me up the stairs. I give her the tour of what is for all intents and purposes, my floor of the house. She loves my room. She saw it before it was decorated.

"Let's have a seat in your office."

"Sure. What's up?"

"I have reports from your doctor and he's very pleased with how well you're doing. Your attorney has also filed a report. The new state attorney has declined to refile the charges against you. So, if you don't get into any trouble, you're free." She smiles.

"Oh, that's great news. Thank you!"

"He'll probably contact you to discuss it, but I got the report right before I left my office, and I couldn't wait to share the good news. There's one other thing I want to talk to you about."

"Okay," my stomach fills with crazy butterflies, my body feels tense, my chest is tight.

"The Henley's have applied to adopt you."

Air gushes from my open mouth. Holy crap! Why didn't they tell me? A million thoughts flutter through my mind. Do I want to be adopted? Do I want them to adopt me? I think I do. The thought of having them as my parents warms my insides. I've been feeling something towards them, mostly gratitude, but it's been growing every day. I might be falling in love with them. They'll be great parents. How crazy is it that me, a murderer, is being asked to join a family who wants to take care of me? Love me? Tears fill my eyes. I'm overwhelmed with emotions that I don't know how to express.

"What are you feeling Violet?" she asks me.

"Ha, I'm not sure how to explain it. But I guess happy covers it."

"So would you be amenable to having them as your adoptive parents?"

"Yes! Absolutely! They're wonderful. Why didn't they talk to me about this?"

"They wanted to make certain it could happen, before they spoke to you to see if you wanted it to happen. I thought it would be best if I discussed it with you first, in case you didn't want to be adopted you could express your feelings without upsetting them. I'm very pleased. They're lovely people and they'll be excellent parents. You're a lucky young lady to find such a wonderful couple who love you."

My eyes snap to hers. "They said they love me?"

"Absolutely dear. They were adamant that they love you and they want you to be their daughter."

Tears stream down my face. "Wow! I can't believe it."

"Believe it. You're a lovely young lady. Your past does not define you. Your history was not your fault, and you endured things no child, or anyone really, ever should. You triumphed in a violent way, but in your circumstances, it may have been the only way." She gets up and leans over me, giving me a hug. I hug her back. I'm changing, for the better, I think. Hugging her doesn't make my skin crawl. It's pleasant.

"The adoption process will take anywhere from three to six months. There'll be an adoption social worker who will help you all through the process, so you won't be seeing me. However, I'll attend your adoption hearing. Do you have any questions?"

"Yeah, can we go find them so I can thank them?"

"Of course, sweetheart, I'll follow you out." I launch myself up and out the door and practically fly down the stairs. I see Xander first, I just about knock him over when I jump on him.

"Whoa! What's up?" I squeeze him tight, and he wraps his arms around me, placing a kiss on top of my head.

"Thank you!" I'm crying again or maybe, still.

"What's wrong?" Emmy enters the room with her eyebrows raised looking between all of us, searching our faces.

"Violet is happy that you want to adopt her, I believe," Mrs. Gonzalez laughs.

I pull away from Xander, and with tears running down my cheeks, I grab Emmy and hug her tight. She bursts into tears and squeezes me too tight in return. But I don't care. We both hug and cry as Xander wraps his arms around both of us. I think he might be crying too when I feel his chest hitch. Mrs. Gonzalez moves to the chair in the corner and sits to wait for us to finish dealing with our emotions. She has a huge smile on her face.

As we break apart and wipe our faces, we join her and sit together on the sofa. She explains all the paperwork and inspections that'll be involved. She says Krewe will be able to handle the adoption which makes me feel comfortable with the process. I know he'll have my back. I bet Joyce will be thrilled about this news, I smirk. I hope I'm there when they tell her.

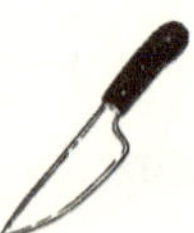

It ends up taking four and a half months for the adoption process. I didn't have to do much, but Emmy and Xander had to complete a huge book of paperwork. We all had emotional evaluations. The house was inspected, twice. Even Copper had to get a checkup at the vet and prove he had all his shots up to date. They said we could bring him to court. This is the first time I've missed a day of school since I started. Dr. Nercy is here, so is Krewe, and Harmony came with Mike. She looks amazing, and she's gained fifteen pounds since I met her. I'm so happy! Even Joyce is here, but only because she promised to behave. I'll believe it when I see it. She had a whole colorful language filled tirade when she heard the news. I must admit, she's been trying to be kinder to me. I'll be her only grandchild after all.

"Will the prospective parents please step forward?" Emmy and Xander step up to the bench. I'm holding my breath next to Krewe at our table.

"I understand you have petitioned the court to adopt Miss Violet Andrea Parades. Do you wish to proceed?"

"We do," they reply simultaneously.

"Do you understand that you will be responsible for the care of Miss Paredes from now until she turns eighteen?"

"We do."

"You're accepting, physical, emotional, mental, and financial responsibility for Miss Paredes. Do you willingly accept this responsibility?"

"We do, your honor," they replied.

"Miss Paredes, please come forward and join the Henley's" I stiffly stand and move to their side. Emmy takes my hand.

I look up at the judge, he's a kind looking older gentleman in a black robe. He's not a monster, and I've never seen him before. Thank God.

"Miss Paredes, even though you've been emancipated, you may be adopted by the Henley's, if you agree."

"Yes, sir, your honor, I agree," my voice trembles.

"Very good. I have read all the documents. I understand you wish to change your name to Violet Andrea Henley?"

"Yes, your honor, that's correct." Emmy moves me between her and Xander, they each hold my hands.

"Okay folks, everything is in order. I'll sign it now," he uses his pen. "There we go, you are officially adopted Miss Henley. Congratulations!"

Both Emmy and Xander hug me. We all cry. The judge has a tear in his eye. Krewe and Dr. Nercy wipe their eyes. Mrs. Gonzalez and my adoption social worker, Mrs. Johnson, both have tears running down their cheeks. Even Harmony has some tears on her face along with a huge smile. Mike is quiet like always. The bailiff walks around passing out tissues. We all wipe our faces and laugh.

"Would you folks like a photo before I head back to my chambers?"

"Absolutely!" Xander answers.

The bailiff takes a photo of just us with the judge. Then the judge says his goodbyes and the bailiff takes a bunch of pictures of all of us with the certificate signed by the judge proclaiming me Violet Henley. I'm floating on air, as this is by far, the best day of my life.

"Do you guys' mind if I call you Mom and Dad?" Emmy hugs me again and her tears well back up.

"Are you kidding? That would be fantastic! You're our daughter now, of course you can call us mom and d-dad," Xander's eyes fill up. This is going to be a tearful day. But it's the best day ever! We all go to Mendo's for lunch to celebrate.

It's a little strange having a new name at school. But in a few days, nobody even notices anymore, it's like I've always been a Henley. I'm ahead in all my classes and I have a perfect GPA. My parents are thrilled with my grades. I love my school. I have some friends, nobody like Harmony, but they make school more fun. We just started the second term of the year. Some of my electives change, but I'm still in computer science. I'm going to take it all year, every year until I graduate.

When I begin eleventh grade, I get a huge surprise. None other than Max, Maximillian Andres Bettencourt III, walks through the door. He's matured since I last saw him in May, when I visited Colby. He looks more like a man and less like a teen. His jaw is wider, his eyes are wiser, his smile is still panty-dropping. He flashes it at me when he sees me. My face breaks into a big smile. Several girls follow his every move with their eyes.

"Violet! Good to see you. I wasn't sure if you'd be here."

"Why didn't you tell me you were out? Or coming to Bayshore?" I asked him.

"I just got out a week ago, didn't know what I was gonna do. My father insisted I return to school. So here I am."

"I'm so happy to see you. What classes are you in?"

"Not computer science!" he chuckles.

"Of course not. Wouldn't want you to fail. How're you doing?"

"I'm great, and glad to see you. Seriously."

We have two classes together and we meet for lunch, every single day. We become closer friends throughout our year of eleventh grade. Max is my constant companion and I like spending time with him. He doesn't pay much attention to anyone else and many of the girls become frustrated when he doesn't acknowledge their advances. I didn't even notice, one of my friends pointed it out.

We laugh a lot. We hang out with Harmony and Mike when we're not at school. They're two years ahead, they aren't in class with us. Max is two years behind where he should be, it puts him in my class. We visit Colby, he remains in Mystic Cross' Center for the rich and unwanted. Colby and I talk daily online, and he teaches me everything he knows about hacking. I teach him everything I learn as well.

When our senior year starts, things are going well for me. My home life is so happy I need to pinch myself. I don't know who's been watching over me lately but they're doing a much better job than the evil fairy godmother of my early life. The only bad thing that happens to me is when Copper gets diagnosed with cancer and we lose him just a month later. My parents offer to get me a new pet, but with college just a short time away I decide I don't want to leave a new pet behind.

My parents are the best. They take me hiking and camping at every opportunity. I learned how to swim, and how to ride a bike in my first year here. They love to hear about my day, every day, and they go out of their way to make plans for all of us so we can spend time together. Emmy teaches me mixed martial arts three times a week. I finally feel like a well-rounded human.

Thankfully, my grandmother, Joyce, doesn't come around much. My mom had to give her an ultimatum, either she must be nice, or she can't come over. She has a very hard time being nice. Not just to me be, but in general. So, she usually chooses to avoid us, which is fine with me. She's not a kind person and she upsets my parents. I don't miss her at all.

We still see Krewe occasionally. Just socially, he's a family friend these days. He got married about six months ago and we went to his wedding. His wife is sweet. They're expecting a baby now.

Dr. Nercy is a close family member despite the lack of blood relation. He still sees me for therapy, but we see him more often for fun. He's still single despite all of mom's attempts to fix him up. He says he just hasn't found the right person yet. He'll figure it out.

When Max and I graduate, we decide to give dating a try. We've been close since he entered my school. Our first romantic kiss happens after our graduation ceremony, our spin the bottle history doesn't count. We're both slated to attend university at Florida State College. My path will be in computer technology and his will be business management. His father wants him to take over the family business. They own a line of luxury hotels and resorts around the world. I think there's fifty-one different locations. His family doesn't like me. His father thinks I'm not good enough for his heir even though he's never even met me.

I'm okay with that, it's his choice, but I won't let anything get in the way of my goals. I've worked hard to recover from my childhood. I graduated Valedictorian of our senior class. I'm the youngest person to do so in the history of the school.

After we celebrate with our friends and families, we have our own celebration on the roof. We smoke weed and talk. We make-out, he hasn't pressured me for anything more. He's solely devoted to me and says he'll wait until I'm ready for intimacy. I'm working on it. I'm fine kissing him, but the thought of more isn't easy, and it gives me anxiety.

I've been doing great for a few years, and this is the final step in my recovery in my mind. If I can be intimate with my boyfriend without having a panic attack, I can officially call myself cured. I'm not sure if I'm more afraid of the act or being healed. I appreciate Max's patience with me. He's amazing. He claims he fell for me the first time he saw me. I can't tell if that's true, but we had an instant connection and he's like a part of me.

I get a job for the summer, for something constructive to fill my time before I leave for college. It's just a simple job at a coffee shop. I've never had a job before, I wanted to get this experience before I leave. Mom and dad bought me a car for my sixteenth birthday for school and if I decided to get a job. Dad made sure I knew how to drive a manual transmission, fix a flat, and change the oil. Working on the cars and his motorcycle was always our special daddy-daughter time. He always makes me laugh with his ridiculous dad humor. He teases me he wanted a child just so he could tell dad jokes.

One day at work when the power goes off after a thunderstorm moves in, it scares the crap out of me when the thunder cracks right outside. I watch out the window as the rain pours from the metal tinted sky. It makes me feel morose. Nothing's as depressing as a dark rainy day. My insides are twisted as the lightning flashes and the thunder rumbles. It brings a feeling of foreboding. I've never liked storms. When I was young there was more than one occasion when I was locked in a dark room alone during a storm. It was terrifying, nobody cared no matter how much I cried. To this day, a storm is the best way to cause me to have a flashback or an anxiety attack, in fact it might be the only way.

When our boss receives word that our power will be off for six hours minimum, she sends us home and closes the shop. I make my way home carefully avoiding the most flooded streets. When I pull into the garage, I'm surprised my parents aren't home yet. Maybe they decided to wait out the storm someplace safe. I decide to put on my pajamas and snuggle under my covers with a book. I wish Copper was still around. He used to be afraid of storms too and we would keep each other company whenever it would thunder.

I check my phone several times waiting for a message from my parents. When the clock strikes 8 p.m. I'm officially worried. I texted them both earlier and they haven't answered. I call each of them and get sent directly to voicemail. Feeling overwhelmed with worry, I decide to call Uncle Randy. Dr. Nercy changed his name to Uncle Randy when I was fifteen. I still see him once a month for therapy, but he's part of my family.

"Hey, Violet, what's up?"

"Hi Uncle Randy, I'm worried about mom and dad. They rode to work together today because mom's car is in the shop. But they aren't home yet, and I can't reach them."

"They probably decided to wait out the storm. Maybe it's interfering with the phone service?"

"I don't know, but I'm very worried, they usually let me know if they're going to be five minutes late."

"Good point. I'll come over and wait with you, we can make some calls. I'll be over in a few minutes."

"Thanks. I'll wait for you downstairs."

"Okay kiddo." He hangs up the phone.

When there's a knock on the door a short time later, I throw open the door for Uncle Randy. My mouth falls open, and two state troopers stand on the steps, their hats are in their hands, their faces somber.

"Miss Henley?"

"Yes?"

"We need to speak with you, are you alone?"

"Yes, why? My uncle is on his way over." Behind them I see headlights as Uncle Randy pulls up the driveway.

"That's him now."

"Let's wait a moment for him to join us," the older trooper says.

I'm frozen to my spot. Uncle Randy runs up the walkway, he shakes the rain from his hair once he's under the portico. They make introductions and Uncle Randy invites them inside.

"Hello. I'm Dr. Nercy. What's going on?" he asks.

"Miss Henley, Dr. Nercy, we're sorry to inform you, there's been an accident."

I don't know what else they said. I fall to the floor and scream from my soul. I don't even notice the tears wetting my cheeks in rivers. I can't breathe. I can't see. Uncle Randy somehow gets me to the sofa, but I'm inconsolable. The troopers leave and Uncle Randy makes some calls. Eventually, Harmony is here, I'm trapped in her arms as I sob. Uncle Randy paces and barks into the phone. Krewe arrives, Max shows up. There's a flurry of activity around me and I can't engage with any of it.

My parents are gone. I'm alone again. I'm devastated. My heart is broken. The only parental love I've ever known is shattered.

Not the end, only the beginning.

Afterword

Thank you for reading. Please leave a review!

Violet's story continues in VioleNt. You can find it here:

https://www.enchantingauthor.com

BOOKS BY E.N. CHANTING

<u>Stories By E.N. Chanting</u>

<u>Forces of Nature Series:</u>

Book One: Force of Corruption (November 2023)

Book Two: Force Majeure (Labor Day 2024)

Book Three: Force of Attraction (Spring 2025)

<u>Southern Suns MC Series</u>

Book One: Ax (Coming 2025)

Book Two: (Orlando)

<u>Violet's Tales- Duet and a half</u>

Book .5: Origin of Violet- Novella (October 2024)

Book One: VioleNt (October 2024)

Book Two: Vile (Spring 2025)

<u>Standalones</u>

Haunted Hunting Camp; A Short Story- Horror (September 2023)

Deadly-Go-Round- Horror (Coming 2025)

The Devil's Affair; A Short Story- Dark Romance (June 2024)

Please sign up for my author newsletter to keep up with new release updates, cover reveals, and giveaways. Subscribe here: https://www.enchantingauthor.com

www.ingramcontent.com/pod-product-compliance
Lightning Source LLC
Chambersburg PA
CBHW030148010826
48973CB00002B/784